With The Pack

Terrie Olsen

Contents

•Chapter 1•

Theadora Sanford•

The first rays of sunshine illuminated my room, which awakened me from my deep slumber. The few moments of clarity when I woke up and realized I was still alive and well brought a smile to my face every time.

I blinked a couple of times to clear the fuzziness. After stretching, I looked at the time; 7:45.

I gasped while running into my bathroom. I showered quickly and put on my normal clothing and brushed my teeth. I ran into the pack kitchen, it was 7:55 and almost wake up time. I hurriedly got out 2 dozens of eggs and pancake batter along with bacon. I began to cook as fast as possible.

Alpha Alexander Kane entered the kitchen along with the beta's son, Bryce Jole. I gulped with wide eyes and faced them. "Where's breakfast?" Alpha Alexander demanded.

"Cooking, master," I replied without stuttering. He hated stuttering and it was too early in the morning for a beating.

"Cooking? It should be done by now!" Beta Bryce snarled venomously. Gulping, I watched Beta Bryce approach me with his hand raised.

"M-my alarm c-cl-clock didn't r-ring" I whispered lowly. I prepared myself for the impact of his slap by closing my eyes. When nothing happened, I opened them and his hand made contact with my left cheek. It held so much power, I fell towards the hot stove and burned my right cheek, and fell to the ground. I screamed in pain as he yanked my elbow upwards, forcing me to stand.

"You know I don't like liars, Thea. You little slut. You've been making excuses for years. I'm tired of all your shit and you need a punishment." He snarled. He dragged me into the hall and I screamed.

"No! Please! It won't happen again!" I sobbed as he pushed me onto the bed of one of the empty rooms. He slammed the door shut and fumbled with his belt. "Please don't!" I begged.

"Shut up!" he growled ripping my clothes off with one brutal force. "I've been nothing but kind as to give you food and shelter and you repay me with this!" He growled forcefully entering his cock inside of me. More tears leaked from my eyes as he continued in a fast manner.

In a matter of minutes, I felt warm on my bare chest and looked down. A white, milk-like liquid oozed down my body slowly. "Clean up," He growled putting his pants back on and exiting the room.

• • •

I looked in the mirror and saw the burn on my cheek was healing, but it left a scar. I put my brown hair into a ponytail and exited my room. I took multiple showers to take off the scent of sex.

I headed up the steps towards the female lounge. On my way, I spotted Amber Hall and Chlöe Tah. "Hey! You!" Amber called out.

I approached them and curtsied, "Yes mistress?" I said looking down at my feet. It was considered an insult for an omega to look someone else in the eye. As if we were too low to look anyone in the eye, even humans. We weren't considered normal wolves because we were labeled weak. I wasn't allowed to shift because of my rank. Even if I could, the other wolves would still abuse me.

"Don't go in my room. Understand?" Amber growled.

"But Alpha said-" I began but she cut me off.

"I don't care what Alpha said. It's my damn room. Do you under-stand?" She snarled.

"Yes mistress," I said low enough for them to hear.

"And give this to Bryce. I swear if you open this, I will kill you!" Chlöe handed me a small piece of paper. It wouldn't matter anyway because I couldn't read.

"Yes mistress," I whispered shuffling away. I began to pick up dirty clothes from the rooms and made sure to avoid Amber's room. After gathering as many clothes as possible, I headed back downstairs towards the laundry room.

I started the first load and headed upstairs to Bryce's room. His room was on the top floor and I had never ever been there. I smelled his scent and heard moaning making me think twice. He hated when I entered on one of his 'sessions'.

I slowly opened the door and closed my eyes. There were 2 females doing things with one another on the screen. Bryce was doing weird things to himself. He was rubbing up and down on 'it' making me gasp. What's happening?

"What are you doing?" He snarled pressing a button on a remote and the screen flew upwards. I looked at the floor, afraid of what he would do. "Why are you crying?" He growled. I couldn't stop the tears from falling out of my eyes. I was afraid of him and everyone. I was raised to serve everyone and respect them. I was always given food if I did as told and it was enough to get by. "Speak now or you get nothing to eat!" He shouted.

I shakily got out the paper and walked over to hand it to him, "I-I'm sorry. It's just.... I..." I began mumbling nonsense and he slapped me.

"What did I say about stuttering?" He barked. I hissed in pain and stood back up.

"Not to do it," I said spilling my tears.

"You are getting no food today. Get out of my face you disgraceful mutt!" He pushed me out and slammed the door shut. I stood up and shuffled back to my room. It was a small room in which I obtained at the age of 8. Also, the age mama died. She was also an omega, nothing more, nothing less.

My room had a small opening in my closet for my pet. His name was Cat and he was a munchkin. "Meow," He purred quietly, peeking his head out.

"Hey, Cat," I whispered kissing his furry head. "Sorry, buddy, no shares today," I told him referring to food. I shared my food, or at least the crumbs, I earned with Cat.

"Meow." He licked my face and I set him down on the floor. I crawled under my bed and took out my first aid kit to treat my burn.

Mama taught me how to tend to different wounds. I applied the aloe vera cream on it and covered it with a bandage. After I finished, I put it back in its original position under my bed.

I changed into my pajamas and got into the bed. The covers were really thin and it was near winter, therefore I would be freezing. I had to be careful not to catch a cold. I closed my eyes and prayed just like mama taught me and fell asleep.

•Joshua Wiley•

I studied the others closely. 'We're nearly there,' Kara said through mindlink. Her voice held hope but I knew the truth. We had to fight for our freedom. Sighing, I followed the rest of the group. My paws collided with the ground making a Thump! Thump! sound.

My ears were perked for any signs of danger, and I was on guard. Prepared for any danger that lies ahead. 'Let's stop for a bit and take a break' Zeke came to a complete stop and I followed along. We each went behind a tree and I placed my backpack on the ground and shifted.

I unzipped my backpack and put on my clothes. I combed my hair a bit with my fingers and sniffed the air. Food! I thought to myself, following the delectable scent. I was the best hunter and fastest in our group. It was only 5 of us: Kara, Zeke, Marshall, Liam, and I.

We were wolves that were left behind after our packs were attacked, forced to become rogues. I've been a rogue ever since I was 2. I try to forget about my family, even though I remembered every detail of their death. It's a weakness I shouldn't have, and trying to remember them will slow me down. As a rogue, I need to be prepared for any possible danger and never have a weakness. That's the way it is, that's the way it always is.

I spotted a deer drinking from a pond. Its tongue cupped the water inside of its mouth. It hadn't noticed me because of my stealth. Creeping towards it, I pulled out my blade and examined it closely. It had big, coal-like eyes that held no emotion but curiosity.

I threw the knife right at its chest, and at first, it didn't respond. After I counted 4 seconds, it fell to the ground with a thud. Bingo! No human would be able to do that unless they had the strength. I approached the animal and made sure it wasn't breathing. When no air left its body, I began to skin him.

• • •

"Mmmm, you really know how to cook deer," Zeke greedily dug into his food.

"Takes some practice," I replied eating a piece of the cooked deer meat. I set up a fire after I cut the deer meat and cooked it. We had a small camp without tents. We had blankets spread out as a makeshift bed and a single fire from nearby branches and leaves.

I smacked a mosquito away and patted my stomach, "I'm gonna go to sleep. Whoever guards, make sure to let the fire die down a bit to not attract attention." I yawned. Marshall nodded and I got into my blanket. It was small but big enough to cover most of my body. I had to make sure my temperature maintained, and I shifted enough to do so. It was getting close to winter and snow would coat the ground soon.

My eyes grew heavy. The group and I were off to north pack territory. We were in search of a new place to live, but any rogue that wanted to be in or out of a pack had to fight for it. And when you fought, you had to fight hard. I'm prepared, right? Leaving the question hanging in my mind, my eyes shut and I fell into a dark abyss.

•*Chapter 2*•

Theadora Sanford•

I woke up with a ball of fur curled next to me. Cat normally doesn't sleep in his little room, He likes to sleep beside me. I don't really know how he makes it all the way up here. I slowly got out of bed and noticed I was up earlier than usual. It was Sunday and most of the members were grumpy about school being tomorrow. I was never allowed to attend school. I wish I could! I want to learn to read, and do math! I always see the complicated problems but I love to solve things.

Everyone refers to the school as a bad thing, but I hadn't been allowed out of the pack house ever since I was born. I never made friends or had anyone to love besides mama. I never knew my father, mama didn't like to talk about him.

I took a shower, got dressed, and brushed my teeth. Just the usual.

I entered the kitchen after my daily routine and began to cook.

• • •

"Master." I bowed to Beta Bryce who sat down and began to eat. Alpha Alexander sat down as well and began to do so.

"Here." Alpha Alexander threw me a piece of bacon. It fell on the dirty ground and I picked it up and hurried to my room. I cleaned it off a bit and split it in half.

"Cat," I whispered entering my room.

I heard a soft, "meow," on my bed and his head poked out of the cover.

"We have food," I grinned giving him the bacon. He licked the bacon first, then took a small bite. He eventually finished it and hopped from the bed and lapped water from his bowl.

I ate the bacon slowly to let the flavor last longer. Cat rubbed my legs and meowed slowly. I realized he hadn't been outside in a while. I grabbed my stool and stood on it. My room was in the basement and my window was high up. I had to go on a stool to reach it. When I found Cat, I made a method with the bushes covering my window. I cut it every once in a while so that it was easy to just push back and forth. I unhooked the window and opened it.

The cold air hit me, making me shiver. I pushed the bushes back, revealing the acres of green grass that were lightly covered in snow. Cat loved snow. I picked him up and let him roam outside. I kept my window open so that he could come back in whenever.

I exited my room to begin my chores. Most pack members were home doing their homework. When I realized I had no chores, I spent my time exploring the house. I rarely got to do it. I would do it more often when I was younger, but that was when Mama was alive. I began to work when she died. Sighing, a frown appeared on my face. I missed Mama. She had green eyes and black hair. We shared the same hair but not the same eyes. Mine were blue and Mama said that it was the color of my papa's eyes. She never told me who he was, just that I had his eyes.

I entered the library and gasped at the variety of books. It was really amazing! The entire place was filled with books. No one entered the library except Alpha Alexander when he had pack work. Most pack members weren't interested in this kind of stuff. Mama loved to read. She read to me a lot when I was little. The only time anyone actually came in here was to use a book for a school project. I remembered mama's favorite book was Little Women. I would cry every time she read it to me. I didn't prefer the movie because I like the setting and people how they are in my imagination rather than a screen.

I looked through the many shelves and picked out a random book. It had the words: G-R-E-A-T E-X-P-E-C-T-A-T-I-O-N-S. I stared at it in wonder, imagining on my own what the book would be about. I wished that I could read. I heard someone clear their throat from behind me and I jumped in shock. The book fell out of my hands in the process.

"A-Alpha," I stammered facing him. His black eyes were hard and filled with hatred.

"What are you doing?" He growled. I put the book back with wide eyes.

"I'm sorry. I was just-" He cut me off.

"Out." I wasted no time in exiting the library. He slammed the door shut from behind me and I ran back downstairs. Cat was already inside, so I slid the bushes back to their original position and closed my window. Cat was covered in snow making me giggle.

"You are just too cute, Cat." I grinned at the mini fur ball. He meowed in response and I sat on my bed. It creaked under my weight and I sighed while laying on my back. Cat meowed and went back to his miniature bedroom.

I decided to take a nap, so I put my hands together and prayed. I smiled while closing my eyes and speaking, "Sleep well, mama."

•Joshua Wiley•

We finally reached the pack territory line and took a break. This would all come crashing down but I had a feeling in my gut this was a bad idea, but something else would become good of it.

"Come on." Kara held a water bottle in front of me. I grabbed it and chugged down the water. I would need to be prepared for this. I waited patiently to see if anyone was doing rounds first. All we wanted was to talk to the alpha for an agreement to join their pack. If not, we would enter their territory without permission.

When no one came, I decided to take action. I stepped onto their territory. The only sound heard was my feet crunching against the small layer of snow on the ground. Everyone followed after me, and we began to walk towards the pack house. I spotted something small moving in the snow and followed it. The thing almost looked like a very tiny cat. I stared at it in confusion. Why was there a cat? I blinked, and the cat disappeared. I must be seeing things.

"Why are you on my land?" An outraged voice barked. I turned, but only to be met with black eyes. "Rogues." He snarled hatefully.

"We come here for peace. We want to be in your pack," Marshall stated proudly.

"Peace? Your kind never wants peace. If you want peace, you have to fight for it," he growled. "Go ahead, fight," ordered the man. "Once they die, burn their bodies." He explained walking away. I knew all my life, I would never forget those hateful black eyes.

The pack members growled at us and we growled back. We all shifted, not caring about our bags. The others shifted as well and attacked.

I was jumped by 2 wolves. One bit into my right shoulder, the other into my side. I threw them off with a shake of my body. They flew to the ground but got ready to launch again. My blood painted the white snow. I attacked one, but another came and bit me repeatedly on my back and tail. I choked back a whimper and a white wolf, that nearly blended into the snow, attacked me. It viciously tore at my body. My fur was matted with blood. My brown fur looked practically red.

I felt myself becoming dizzy, and I fell to the ground with a thud.

•Theadora Sanford•

I woke up shivering. I wasn't able to sleep. Cat was covered in snow, and I knew he went back out. I chuckled and got up to step on the stool. I was about to close the window when I saw a violent scene. Wolves were attacking each other. There was a lot of blood, growling, and snarls. 4 of them were dead, and they began to attack a brown wolf. I gasped at the horrific scene. The brown wolf finally dropped to the ground and the other wolves left.

Once they were out of sight, I climbed out of the window and ran to each wolf and checked for a heartbeat. 4 of them were gone, but there was a faint one from the brown wolf. I grabbed his fur and began to pull him towards the house, but I was too weak. Cat appeared beside me and clamped his small mouth on his fur and tried to help me pull, but with no such luck.

"Nice try," I said to Cat who only meowed in response. The brown wolf stirred a bit until it shifted. He was male with dark brown hair. I wasn't able to see his eyes because they were closed. "Sir?" I said. He moved a little, but I found it easier to carry him.

"My bag.... the black one." He grumbled weakly. I looked around for his bag.

"Cat, take his bag inside," I said pointing to the black one. Cat obeyed instantly and I began to speed up my thought process. They were going to come soon. I grabbed his arm and managed to pull him towards the window. There was a blood trail, so I quickly wiped it away with the snow. I put the man inside my room and shut the bushes and my window.

"It hurts," he groaned.

"I'm sorry about that." I bit my lip while taking out my first-aid kit and spraying him with a scent masker before sealing his wounds. They would take a while to heal, but he would most likely make it. I dragged him into Cat's room to make sure he stayed hidden. I was dead if I were to get caught.

"Sir, my name is Thea. You need to rest." I demanded because he was moving too much.

"Thea," he repeated as if testing my name.

"Gift," He whispered. I stared at him in confusion. "Your name.... It means gift." He repeated before completely blacking out.

•Chapter 3•

Theadora Sanford•

I packed the strange man's clothes into his bag after folding them. I washed them before because they were dirty. My heart was beating so loudly that I was able to hear it. Why didn't those people help the man? He was dying! Did they leave him like that on purpose? Did I do something wrong?

It was late at night, and everyone was asleep. I was able to hear Alpha Alexander shouting at the men that they lost something. I decided to go to sleep so I wouldn't be tired in the morning. I slowly crept to my bed and got inside my blanket. I said my prayers and Cat jumped into the bed with me. I let him curl up and I smiled softly while closing my eyes.

• • •

My alarm rang, successfully waking me from my sleep. I made sure that I was up early to make sure the man was okay. I got into the shower and washed off. Afterwards, I brushed my teeth and washed my face. I smiled at my reflection and ran into the room. "Sir." I whispered softly. He stirred a bit. Most of his wounds had healed. "Sir," I repeated poking him.

His eyelids flew open, and I was met with beautiful grey eyes. I had never seen anyone with grey eyes. It was an amazing first experience for me. I quickly looked away before he was able to notice and stared at the ground. "Wh.....what's going on?" He groaned.

"I-I helped you. You were dying," I replied.

The man questioned, "Your name..... It's Thea, right?"

"Yes sir."

"Why do you call me sir? My name is Joshua, but call me Josh." He greeted. "And why are you looking at the ground?"

His question took me off guard, but I answered, "I-I was raised to. I-I'm an omega." Josh grabbed my chin gently and raised my head so that I was staring into his beautiful eyes again.

"Well, I'm a rogue. Rogues don't need to be treated specially." He shrugged. I nodded slowly. I heard a soft meow and fur press up against my body. I smiled while picking up Cat. "Who's that?" Josh asked.

I placed Cat on his stomach, "My cat. His name is Cat."

"Cat the cat." Josh chuckled. I loved that sound. Laughter. It reminded me of Mama's laugh. All the jokes we shared. I smiled sadly. "Thea? Are you okay?" Josh interrogated with concern. I avoided his gaze, my eyes instinctively found their way back to the ground.

"I-I'm sorry. I-I was j-ust-"

"Why are you sorry? You don't have to be afraid to smile." He stated in confusion while tilting my head upwards towards his gaze. "It's okay, really. I'm really thankful you saved my life."

"You're welcome. I'ts just that master doesn't like when I-I smile or look him in the eye. It's disrespectful b-because I'm just an omega."

I tried to stop myself from stuttering, but I wasn't able to. "You're treated that bad here? I'm really sorry about that. Most omegas aren't treated this badly from my past experiences." Josh frowned sadly.

I took a glance at my clock. "I have to cook breakfast for everyone. Please try not to draw attention." I begged him.

"Don't worry, I can't go anywhere with my leg bandaged up," he noted.

I got up and shut the door to the small room, but left a crack. I ran into the kitchen, just in case anyone was there. No one was, so I began to cook.

• • •

"What did I say about putting this shit on my plate?" Alpha boomed. His dark eyes filled with hate and disgust. "What are you looking at?" He snarled making me drop my eyes to the floor.

"I-I forgot." I stuttered. Alpha dropped the chocolate pancakes and bacon on the floor.

"You better not forget next time, girl. Clean this shit up and get out of my sight." He shouted slapping me. I began to clean up, ignoring the stinging on my cheek. After finishing, I ran back down to my room and shut my door. I covered my eyes with my hands and began to cry. Why can't I do anything right?

Because you're useless, Thea! No one likes you! You will forever be alone and Mama is gone! She left you, too! I reminded myself, but I only cried harder.

"Thea," A voice called, and I suddenly remembered Josh in the room. I wiped away my tears and opened the closet door. He stared at me with concern.

"I'm fine," I whispered. Josh frowned and traced something on my cheek.

"Who did that? You were slapped?"

"Yes. I-I forgot alpha is allergic to chocolate but I put them in the pancakes!" I mumbled.

"It's okay. We all make mistakes," he said gently.

"It's just, everything I do is wrong. Bringing you here was wrong." I began to cry again.

"It wasn't wrong. Sometimes the hardest thing is the right decision."

I seemed to calm down afterwards. I felt some sense of comfort from Josh. "Thank you," I whispered.

"Hey, it was no problem." He smiled at me.

"Josh?" I said staring at the ground again. My voice was quiet.

"Yeah?" He asked.

"What did you mean by gift?"

He shrugged, "Your name. It means gift. You know, a blessing or miracle."

"How do you know?" I asked as he tilted my head up again.

"I don't really know. It's just something I remember from my past." He shrugged. "Anyways, who do you live with?" He asked, seeming to dodge the subject.

"It's just me and Cat. My mama died when I was 8." I said, my voice dropping at the mention of her.

"Oh, I'm sorry to hear that. How old are you?"

I thought for a second if I should reply or not. "16. I turn 17 2 weeks from now." I finally answered.

"I'm 18." He replied. Woah, he was old. I think. Josh spotted the black bag beside him and tried to grab it, but I laid him back down gently.

"You shouldn't do it. I'll get it." I grabbed the bag.

"Can you take out the bottle with Tylenol on it?" He asked. I nervously began to look in the bag. "Do you see it?" He asked. I shook my head. I couldn't read, but how would I tell him that?

"I-I can't find it b-because I can't read," I said lowly. I prepared myself for his laughter and "You stupid girl," but got nothing.

He lifted my head up again, "Really?" He asked in concern. I nodded slowly.

"I only know how to read and spell my name." I whispered softly, "My mama taught me."

I felt embarrassed to tell him this. "I can," he offered. I looked at him in confusion. "I can teach you how to read."

My eyes became wide and a smile grew on my face. "Really?" I whispered.

"Of course," he confirmed giving me a lopsided smile. I felt my heart skip and I knew the perfect thing to start off with.

"Wait here," I said getting up.

"I couldn't move even if I wanted." He chuckled.

"Right." I laughed lowly and opened one of the drawers. I grabbed a paper and pencil and searched the bottom of the drawer. I blew away the dust and picked it up. It brought back memories about mama. The happy ones. I grinned while bringing it back to his small room. He scooted over a bit and patted the space beside him. I scooted next to him and he held the book in front of us. "It was my mama's favorite book; Little Women. She would read it to me as a child." I told him.

"Your mother sounds amazing," he said. I nodded.

"So I know my ABC's, just not to pronounce it." I explained. He began to write the Alphabet on the blank paper. Once he was done, he pointed at the A.

"A makes an ah sound."

"ah," I repeated after him.

"Good, now the b sounds like buh." He pointed to the capital B.

"Buh," I said. I hadn't realized it, but I was leaning on his shoulder. He smiled at me.

"Good job." He then began with the next letter.

• • •

"Now how do you say this?" He asked writing down a three letter word.

I sounded it out in my mind, "Cat." I replied.

"Good, now spell it."

"C-A-T. Cat." I said proudly.

"Good job. It's getting late," he yawned. I nodded and got up with the book in my hand.

"Thanks a lot, Josh.... For helping me read"

"You're welcome. It's the least I could do after you saved me from certain death." He chuckled. I laughed and got into my bed. I put my hands together and prayed.

"Night, Josh. Night, mama." I whispered before dozing off.

•Chapter 4•

Theadora Sanford•

I let the blaring of my alarm clock wake me. It was like any normal day. I wiped my eyes and got out from bed. My heart dropped at the empty room, where Cat was curled into a ball, but Josh was gone. The bandage on his leg was cut off by what looked like a knife, and it was lying inside the room.

I frowned while walking to it. Mama's book was still there, but Josh and his bag were gone. I swallowed a lump in my throat. It was only a matter of time before he left me as well. I shrugged it off, there was no point in trying to make friends. I still had Cat.

I took a shower and checked myself in the mirror and smiled at my reflection. I chuckled a little and walked out of the the bathroom and into my room. I inhaled the delicious scent of meat and my eyes landed on Josh. "Hungry?" He asked.

I examined the meat closely. "What is it?" I asked breaking off a piece.

"Deer meat."

I gasped, "People eat deer?"

"So what? People eat pigs, cow, and chicken. Deer is pretty good." Josh ate the meat. I smelled it again as if it were poisoned. "Come on, there's a first for everything." He nudged my side while wiggling his eyebrows.

I hesitantly took a bite. The flavor instantly exploded in my mouth, and I loved it instantly. "This is delicious!" I moaned grabbing another piece.

• • •

Alpha Alexander and Beta Bryce didn't come down for breakfast, which was odd. But Luna Erica did. She glared at me while sitting down at the table. She was as cruel as Alpha Alexander, and Beta Bryce.

"Good morning," I whispered placing her plate in front of her.

"Shut up!" She snapped. "Get out of here you filthy piece of shit." She growled. I bowed and left. At least she didn't hit me. I made my way upstairs towards the male hallway. It was their laundry day and it was frightening to be in that part of the pack house.

"You!" Gamma Charlie's son, Matthew, waved me over. I rushed towards him.

"Sir?" I asked staring at the ground.

"Can you do me a favor and go upstairs and tell Alpha Alexander that we have more information?" He asked, although it was an order to me. He wasn't mean to me or nice. He was just respectful and never hurt me. His voice was always calm.

"Yes sir." I shuffled away, repeating his words in my head, so that I wouldn't forget. I went up the steps slowly. I hoped that it wasn't a bad time, or they would be very upset with me. I heard shouting the closer I got towards Alpha's office.

"You..... No...... Baby!" I heard Beta Bryce shout, but could only catch some words.

"Don't... First.... Alpha!" Alpha Alexander shouted back at Beta Bryce.

"No choice....give..... Me." Beta Bryce said in a more calm manner. I lightly knocked on the door. Alpha Alexander answered. His black eyes were swimming with small golden flecks, indicating his wolf near to surfacing.

"What?" He snarled at me.

"Future Gamma Matthew said that they have more information." I told him.

"Okay, now go." He slammed the door on my face. They began to talk lowly and I wasn't able to hear. I headed back to the male hall. They weren't swarming everywhere because it was a school day. Most of everyone were at school.

"Hey, Thea, I did the other clothes for you. You don't have to do the laundry today." Matthew said.

I gave him a small nod, "Yes sir. Thank you, sir."

"You're welcome. You have free time now." He explained. I nodded and walked away.

•••

"Now read and spell it."

"Josh. Capital J-o-s-h." I said.

"Why capital J?"

"Because it's your name."

"Good job. That's perfect. Now write it."

He handed me the pencil and I wrote it against the paper as nice as I was able to. It was really crooked and squiggled because I hadn't written in a long time. "Is it okay? I mean.... I still need to practice my penmanship and all..."

Josh chuckled, "It's good. You're a fast learner, and practice does make perfect."

I smiled, "I like your handwriting better. It looks neater." I tilted my head as he wrote Josh below my writing.

"You think so?" He asked.

"Mhm." I nodded and heard Cat meow. I turned to him and picked the tiny ball of moving fur up. "Hey Cat!" I giggled.

He meowed in response and licked my cheek. "Hey um, Thea...." Josh tilted his head.

"Yeah?" I grinned putting Cat down.

"I like your eyes." He smiled.

I blushed and turned away, "Thanks." I replied. I stared at the ground, I didn't want Josh to see my rosy red cheeks. He lifted my chin anyways.

"You don't have to look down, remember?"

I nodded, "I know."

Josh rubbed my cheek, "That scar..." He sighed. "What they do to you is wrong." I felt weird at him mentioning my pack. "You know that Thea, don't you?" He questioned. I stared at the ground, not answering him. "Thea." He repeated in a softer tone.

"I'm sleepy." I made up an excuse and walked into my room.

"Are you mad?"

"No." I got into the covers as he got into the other side of my bed, scooting closer to me because of it's size. "It's just..." I turned around and faced him. "I grew up here my entire life. And you're a... " I gulped. I didn't want to upset him.

"A what, Thea?" He growled narrowing his eyes. He was angry at me, and I was afraid.

"I didn't mean to upset you." I apologized dropping my eyes to the ground.

Josh approached me and held my chin up, examining my face, "I'm not mad Thea." He sighed. "You shouldn't be afraid to say it. I'm a rouge. It's the truth, and it doesn't hurt." He stated blankly.

"And your kind doesn't help people like me. Wh-why do you want to help me. I'm a sixteen year old omega that's given nothing." I gulped.

Josh frowned, "Because I've been through the same thing. I saw it... Your emotions just from one look in your eyes, and you reminded me of me when I was a kid. Alone, out to fend for myself. I can help you, Thea. My group was killed after we tried to come to this pack, but I can take you away from all of this. The sadness, fear, pain, the isolation." His eyes sparkled as he spoke. "Do you want to be free, Thea?"

A frown took over my face. Of course I wanted to be free. I didn't want to be alone either, but this oppurtunity was more than I could chew. I grew up here. This is where my best and worst memories were held. And I felt like leaving would only make matters worse. What about Cat? Where will we sleep? Clothes? Food? What I had here was enough to get by. I was given enough to eat and drink, and I was given clothes and shelter. No matter how bad they treated me, I was still thankful for what I had. For what they gave me. "Josh," I started. The smile being wiped off from his face by my expression. "I'm sorry."

His face became stone again, and he silently stood up, "I understand." was the only thing he said as he turned off the light and got into his own room. I really liked Josh being my friend, but he couldn't be here forever. He would have to leave eventually.

We were both awake, but none of us dared to speak. Least to say, it was an awkward silence.

•••

I woke up late in the morning. I didn't have to prepare breakfast, because another pack was visiting. I took a quick shower and washed myself off. I walked over to Josh silently and sat down in front of him. He was so handsome when he was sleeping. I found myself staring at his features.

"Josh." I whispered poking his face. "Josh." I repeated. He looked alert when he opened his eyes, towering over my small frame and his eyes darkening. I laughed slightly nervous and scooted out from underneath him. "There's no danger." I assured him.

"It's instinctive." He shrugged. "You hungry?"

I nodded and he got out of the bed, "Where are you going?" I asked when he put on his shoes.

"Hunting. I'll be back in about 30 minutes. Maybe less."

"Oh." I got up and walked into the bathroom. My face looked different. There was something that changed, but I couldn't tell what it was. That was until I noticed my smile. A real smile. Not one to assure myself that I was okay when I wasn't. My face was brighter, not in it's sickly pale state. I blinked to make sure I wasn't daydreaming, but to my shock I wasn't. I felt like I was digging back in my history. The same look when Mama was alive.

•••

"Master." I bowed.

Beta Bryce waved his hand, "Just stand right there against the wall." He ordered.

"Are you sure she's not gonna spill anything?"

"No one will listen to her. She will be punished either way. Thank you for the concern Alpha Xavier."

I stood against the wall, my mind replaying my breakfast with Josh. He made a special meal just for the two of us. He was a great friend, and I was really glad to have him. "Alright, down to business." Alpha Xavier stated.

"Ah, yes. After I take over as Alpha, I'll need some allies. You, being a powerful alpha will be very helpful."

Alpha Xavier raised his brow, "And why should I be speaking to a beta? This is alpha matters, kid."

"Look, I'm going to be the alpha soon, so that should be enough. It may not be official, but I'm still alpha and I always will be. Now," Beta Bryce cleared his throat. "if we do make an alliance, I guarantee you protection from other packs. I don't understand how you can pass up on an offer like this. This is after all, the most powerful pack."

"Yes, but I do have concerns about war. If I'll be there for you, will you be there for us? And as for your record of taking down packs, I already see a deal forming."

"That shouldn't be a concern, Xavier. I'll definitely be by your side during any wars. But, uh, I do have some conditions."

Alpha Xavier sat back, "And what shall those conditions be."

Beta Bryce stood up, and began pacing, "I get 50 of your best soldiers, your daughter, and your battle strategies."

•*Chapter 5*•

Theadora Sanford•

"What!" Alpha Xavier growled in outrage. He stood up from his seat. I jumped and stepped farther away from the both of them.

"You have my word if you agree to the 3 conditions, you and your pack will be protected."

"You can take my soldiers and my battle strategies, but not my baby!" Xavier snarled furiously at Beta Bryce, who still kept a calm and cool façade.

"I will be king of this pack soon, and every king needs a queen."

"No. Never! The deal is off." Beta Bryce was slightly shocked that Xavier dried his offer.

He narrowed his eyes at Xavier and leaned forward in his seat, "That's the thing, Xave. It isn't a deal until you agree. With the snap of my finger," Beta Bryce snapped his finger. "I could have you dead."

Alpha Xavier narrowed his eyes, "Get out of my sight you filthy piece of shit." Bryce used his enhanced speed to push Xavier in his seat. He cuffed Alpha Xavier to the chair along with it with silver handcuffs. "What are you doing?" Alpha Xavier demanded furiously as he began yanking on the cuffs. Beta Bryce glared at Alpha Xavier. His hard, cold eyes sent shivers down my spine. How was it that one man could be so evil?

"Whore," Beta Bryce turned to me, and I bowed to show him that I was listening. "Bring me the knives." He ordered. The knives? He couldn't kill Alpha Xavier. It was cruel so cruel, even for a person like Bryce. I shakily walked over to Beta Bryce's desk and opened one of the drawers. I took out the dark wooden box box that away so familiar to me, and walked over to Beta Bryce. He snatched it out of my hands and opened it, looking at the wide selection of silver knives displayed in long and short sizes, different varieties and blades.

Alpha Xavier threw me a pleading look. His eyes big, and he glanced at me and then the keys on Beta Bryce's desk. I got his insinuation that he wanted me to free him.

I backed up towards the wall as Beta Bryce picked out a knife. I was fraud of what Beta Bryce would do to me, as well. "I guess I'll have to do this by force. It didn't have to be this way, Xavier." Beta Bryce sighed menacingly.

I couldn't take it anymore! He couldn't kill Alpha Xavier! I needed to help him. I crept unnoticed to Beta Bryce's desk, and I slowly picked up the keys. I was careful not to jingle them at all. Xavier noticed me and turned to Beta Bryce. "You monster!" He shouted, trying to distract Beta Bryce from noticing me also.

Beta Bryce chuckled, "You don't have to state the obvious, Xavier."

"You're going to be a terrible alpha." Xavier narrowed his eyes as I slowly walked forward. My hand slipped and the keys fell to the ground, it seemed to echo throughout the room. Uh oh.

Beta Bryce turned to me, and the fallen keys on the ground. "You betraying bitch! Going against your own alpha!" He barked slapping me. I bit my tongue to stop a scream from leaving. "Fine, since you think you can disobey me, you have to kill him." Beta Bryce gave me the knife.

I shook my head, tears falling out of my eyes, "No, please. I'm sorry!" I begged him.

He chuckled darkly, "Do it, little girl."

He gave me a head start by pushing me towards alpha Xavier. Xavier gave me a pleading look, not to kill him. I couldn't kill him. I couldn't kill anyone or anything. Not even a fly for Pete's sake. "I can't." I sobbed, my bottom lip quivered.

Beta Bryce grabbed my waist tightly, "Kill him, or I kill you."

More tears fell out like a thunder storm, Xavier had finally given up. Without thinking, I stabbed the knife into Beta Bryce's stomach and ran to the keys. Beta Bryce fell to the ground, screaming at the silver and cursing at me. I worked fast, unlocking Alpha Xavier as Beta Bryce pulled the knife out. "Go!" I shouted at Alpha Xavier.

He complied to my wishes by shifting and running out of the room, not glancing back. I ran out of the room just as Beta Bryce recovered. "Stop her!" He ordered running after me, but he wasn't as fast with the silver that weakened him.

I ran downstairs and into my room. I shut my door and locked it. Beta Bryce began to bang on it, "Open up little whore!" He shouted. "Or I will fucking break this door down myself!"

I cried while curling into a ball on the floor. "Thea?" Josh embrace me, his presence seemed to calm me down a little. "What happened?"

I looked up at him, my eyes were blurred with tears. "I did something, Josh. Something bad, and you have to get out of here. Now."

He shook his head, "I don't-"

"If you don't open the door in 3 damn seconds, I will break it down. One..."

Josh picked me up, "I can't leave you with him Thea."

"Two..."

"Josh, just go!" I whispered pushing him into the room and covering it.

"Three!" I ran to the door and unlocked it just in time. Beta Bryce glared at me, grabbing my wrists.

"Ow! You're hurting me!" I cried as he pushed me onto the bed.

"You betrayed me..... Your own alpha!" He growled pinning my wrists to the bed. I fought back, kicking and screaming at him. "Stop fighting!" He shouted lifting up my dress.

"Bryce, that is enough!" Someone demanded. Beta Bryce slowly got off of me, glaring at Alpha Alexander, "She had a reason to do what she did! You chained an alpha to a chair! How else do you think she would react! And you are not alpha and never will be!" He shouted furiously.

Beta Bryce dusted himself off, "Why are you defending her!"

"I'm not defending her. I'm telling you the truth. And as for the alpha title, you will never have it. How do you think your father would react to this? You've gone insane for the alpha title!"

"What are you saying?"

"I have a son. He's been at the Alpha Academy for years. You are not, and never will be alpha!" Alexander stated bitterly.

"But how, how is this possible, where is he?" Bryce demanded.

"You watch who you're talking to, boy." He barked in his alpha voice.

Beta Bryce bowed, submitting to Alpha Alexander, "Yes, Alpha."

"Dad? What's the commotion." A boy, no older than 20 appeared. His eyes were the same color black as Alexander's, his mouth and jaw line were alike in a way, and his hair color was the same as luna Erica's.

Beta Bryce looked at the boy with narrowed eyes. "If not for Jake, I would have you stripped from your title as beta. Now leave this girl and meet me in my office." Alexander said. Jake. Jake was his name. I gulped, having another cruel alpha to face.

But something was weird, Jake smiled at me before leaving. He gave me a real smile. I gulped while looking at the ground, remembering my eye contact rules. Beta Bryce gave me one last glance before walking out of my room, slamming the door on his way.

"Thea." A soft voice called out. I didn't turn to face Josh, until I noticed something glimmering. I turned towards him, spotting a knife in his hand.

"You..... You were going to kill Beta Bryce." I whispered.

He frowned, "I wasn't going to let him hurt you."

"But.... But it's dangerous!"

"I was going to do it to protect you, Thea. Why are you so against it?" He growled.

"He... He's important to the pack. Even if they hate me for who I am, they're still my family."

"Can't you see, this pack isn't right for you!"

"They aren't a pack, they're my pack. And I was born to defend them for life!"

Josh narrowed his eyes, "I can see it in your eyes, the pain, the fear, the sadness. You aren't fooling me."

I shrunk back in defeat, knowing that I couldn't defend myself and my beliefs anymore. "I'm sorry." I whispered.

Josh took the empty space beside me, embracing me in his arms, "No, I'm sorry. I shouldn't have yelled at you." He sighed. "You're only a kid. You don't understand the world yet."

I didn't respond, only letting his warmness consume me. "What you said is right. I've just been trying to hide it for so long."

"I know, but you don't have to hide anything from me. You are who you are, you don't pick how or when you're born. Thea, don't let society destroy you. Be you, because what happens when we all die, and our souls leave our bodies? There will be the dark souls that were beautiful on the outside, and the pure souls that others hated. But this skin on our body doesn't define who we are. Our souls last forever, our flesh doesn't."

•Chapter 6•

Theadora Sanford•

I covered my eyes with my arm and yawned. I realized it was still late and I had just woken up early. I slowly got out of my lumpy bed. Josh was gone, which was odd. I checked the time, only to see that it was 9 at night. Where could he possibly be? Did he always leave around this time of night? Maybe he left for good? A sinking feeling was felt on my stomach area and I sighed. I slowly stalked into my bathroom and splashed water on my face, feeling refreshed. I brushed my hair and put it up into a ponytail.

After drying off, I walked back into my room, noticing my door was open. Someone's scent was around my room as well. "Hello?" A voice called out in the dark. I fumbled for the light, grabbing the string and tugging it. The light illuminated my room, and also the person who was Jake. Why was he here? Did they find out about Josh? My heart began thudding against my chance at the possibility of them finding out about Josh. Maybe that's why Josh was missing so late at night. I cleared my throat and bowed, "Alpha Jake?"

"No need for titles, Miss Sanford, I won't go around calling you Omega Theadora." He chuckled.

I cleared my throat again, "Uh, Jake? Wh-What are you doing here?" I was comfortable not using the manners I was grown up to use. I was used to always using titles, or roles. Whatever they liked to call it.

My eyes were stuck on the ground as he spoke, "There is a ball tommorow in which you must attend. I don't want you to wear a servants clothing, just a normal dress. Alpha Xavier is visiting again, and he wants to specially thank you."

"I... I don't have a dress." I whispered in embarrassment. All the clothes I had were 7 of the same pairs of a dress which were themed black and white and only for the servants of the pack. I had never worn anything else besides that in my entire life.

"Nonsense, I'll let you borrow my card and you can be escorted out to the mall in one of the pack vehicles in the morning."

"But, I-" I began to stutter, but even if I tried, I wouldn't form a complete sentence.

"That's orders from your alpha, understand?" he demanded more firmly.

"Yes sir." I shrunk back.

"Alright then, I'll leave you to it-" He stopped short, smelling the air. "What's the smell?" he inhaled again. His eyes were narrowed, and he seemed to lowly growl.

My eyes expanded, realizing that Josh's scent wasn't covered, "What scent, sir?" I covered pretending I had no idea what he was talking about.

"It smells like..." He sniffed the air, walking around my room. Fear swelled inside of me and I begged in my mind he wouldn't find anything. "Nah, there's no possible way. My nose must be playing tricks on me." He chuckled. I let out a silent breath of relief. That was a close one. Too close. "Now, where were we? Oh, yes, I'll have pack guards escort you to and from the mall. I guess I'll be on my way then." he grinned, "Goodnight." he smiled at me.

I nodded, "Goodnight, sir." I exhaled as he left the room, shutting the door behind him. That was way too close. If he found out Josh was being harbored and nurtured back to health by an omega, I would surely be killed.

I sighed and got rid of those thoughts. At least I didn't get caught. Instead, I was invited to a ball! I couldn't even see me at a big and fancy party attending as one of the guests. I had never even seen a ball. I was only left to clean up afterwards, and imagine what it was like. A dress? Shopping? Me? I was so caught up in my thoughts that A scent filled my nose, and it smelled delightful. Josh appeared climbing inside my room with agility, a bag in one hand as he closed back the window. "Mmmmm!" I inhaled, smelling the scent.

Josh chuckled, "It's just McDonald's, you know?"

I tilted my head, sitting on my bed with my legs crossed. "Mac what?"

He looked at me in astonishment, "You don't know what McDonald's is?" He sat in front of me and took everything out of the bag.

"Nope. Is it a type of food?"

Josh chuckled again, "It's a restaurant. A drive thru resturaunt." He handed me one of the wrapped things in yellow paper and I stared at it.

"I'm supposed to eat the paper?"

Josh rolled his eyes, "You're supposed to take the paper off." He unwrapped it for me, and I felt like an idiot.

I stared at the burger. "It's just a burger." I laughed.

He took a bite of his, "Try it." He said with a full mouth. Shrugging, I bit into the burger. It was the most awesome moment of my life.

"Wow!" I closed my eyes and chewed. "Where did you get this." I took another bite and chewed.

"You, my friend, have a world to explore." Josh began. He wrapped his arms around my neck and I leaned on his shoulder. "Earth is actually a beautiful place, it's just some humans don't know how to treat it. Not all of us, but I would say a majority," "but there are so many places you haven't been. Rome, Greece, Paris, New York."

"What's it like? Have you been there?" I asked hopefully.

"I wish. I just don't have the money for a luxurious boat ride. But I've heard a lot about them." he smiled and I closed my eyes as I imagined each one.

"Can you tell me?" I questioned, needing a better visual.

"Ah, where do I start?" he sighed in satisfactory and snapped his fingers, "Paris! The city of love..."

•Chapter 7•

Theadora Sanford•

"Wake up, miss." A soft voice called out. I slowly opened my eyes and they met with light brown ones. "Your limo is prepared, and so are your guards." The girl with pretty eyes told me.

I slowly nodded and sat up as she left my room. I heard a couple of groans before Josh pulled back the blanket on the wall. "Good morning." I giggled. Cat rubbed his face on my arm, purring softly.

"Morning." He replied huskily. "What was she talking about?" he questioned cautiously. I rubbed Cat and picked him up.

"Just shopping for a dress. I'm going to a ball." a smile on my face, I had heard of them, but never went to one.

"A ball? Since when are omegas attending those?" he stretched.

"The future alpha wants to thank me for saving his life.... From master Bryce."

Josh smiled encouragingly, "That's great, Thea." The way he looked at me made my heart do skips. I couldn't help but smile back and hug him.

"I'm so happy. This is my first ball!" I squealed lifting Cat and hugging him too. I kissed his soft fur before letting him roam and smiling brightly at Josh. I couldn't wait to find the perfect gown, and be in the same room as another alpha. It was all new to me, and a rare experience for omegas.

His smile faltered a little and I detected something was wrong. "A-Are you alright?" I asked slightly worried.

"Of course I'm alright." he chuckled and the spark returned in his eyes. "Go on, I'll just be here all day." he shrugged.

"Could you, uh, take care of Cat for me?" I asked hesitantly.

"Yes, of course."

I ran over and hugged him again, "Thanks, Josh!" I ran into the bathroom as fast as I could and did my business in there before running out and rushing upstairs.

At the dining room, Misty, Sophie, and 2 other girls I'd never seen around were gathered and eating. They ignored me as they chatted away. I sat down stunt usual spot in the corner of the room and waited. I wasn't allowed to eat unless I was told I could. I closed my eyes and placed my head on my knees. "Thea? What are you doing down there?" A familiar voice questioned. I looked up and realized it was Jake.

I quickly forced my eyes away from him, remembering my eye contact rule. "Just waiting to eat." I tried to make it sound less not like a mumble.

"Why waiting? C'mon, you can sit beside me." he smiled and held out his hand for me to take. I flushed as I grabbed his hand and we both sat down at the table. The girls grew quiet as they glanced at me. Some of them scooted down and I pretended not to notice.

Jake asked for another plate, and a maid soon came out with one and placed it in front of me. Everyone went back to eating and chatting, and I began to eat. I tried to hold back a pleasured groan as the flavor of the food exploded on my tongue. It was much better than MacRonald's.

They ate this delicious food everyday? (Although it was my cooking most of the time). All I had was spoiled leftovers that always had mold, and no food at all from time to time. Everyone took what they had for granted. If I were a normal pack member, I would never any of it for granted. They were privileged to even have food at all. "Did you enjoy it?" Jake asked as soon as I was finished.

"Yes sir, it was delicious." I shyly mumbled.

"It's about time you ladies head off. Be back in an hour." Jake firmly ordered. Ladies? As in more than one? I wasn't going alone? Sophie, Misty, and the other 2 girls stood up and made their way out the door. I quickly stood up and followed after them. "Bye Thea, have fun." Jake waved.

"Bye." I whispered giving a small wave back.

•••

The entire limo drive was very quiet on my account. Sophie, Misty, and the other 2 girls whose names I had learned were Emily and Lola were forced to sit in the same part of the limo as me. Each of us got a personal body guard for protective uses. The 4 girls acted as if I didn't exist, but I didn't mind because my entire life no one actually acknowledged my presence unless they needed me to do something for them.

When we parked into the lot of the "mall" I grew nervous. I didn't know what a mall was, or what it held. For all I knew, it was a trap. I slowly got out the limo after all the other girls. They began walking off with their guards without me.

"Hey, guys, wait up." I called out as I ran as fast as I could to catch up, only to run into my body guard. I heard them laugh at me, and I grew embarrassed as they kept walking.

"Don't let them get to you." My guard said as he checked over me for injuries. We began walking once he realized that I was okay.

"I-It doesn't bother me." I nearly whispered. "Plus, everyone says that. At least, everyone that cares." I let out a sigh. He said nothing after that as we walked into the mall. My eyes grew big as I stared about. People. There were people. Human people. I slowed down and felt like hiding behind my body guard. Humans scared me. Some were evil. They killed their own because of jealousy, anger, hatred, love, or envy. It was the first time I encountered not only one, but so many. The times a werewolf made interactions with a human were if they were mates, or if it were a hunter.

"Don't be afraid," my body guard whispered low enough for only me to hear.

"Hey, Thea, come on!" Misty suddenly turned around and waved me over. I looked up at my body guard, and he gave me an assuring nod. I held in my excitement of finally being let into something stay inside of me as I rushed over. "Let's find you a dress first. They might have some at Forever 21, wanna check it out?" Misty asked. She smiled warmly at me.

I grinned, "Yeah, sure!" I accidently squeaked. She hooked her arm in mine and she giggled as we made our way into the store she considered "Forever 21."

"Let's be friends. All of us." Sophie smiled as she took my other arm and led me down another issue filled with beautiful dresses. "Ooh, this one would look really good on you." She tugged on a bright green dress. It just didn't look.... Me.

"Or maybe this!" Lola ran up with a red dress. "I can do your hair and makeup for you!" She smiled. "Go ahead and try it on," she insisted helping me into the changing room. I closed the door after she left and locked it. "I hope it's the right size. It was the only one left," she added as I took off my servant dress. I looked away at my body in the mirror. There were so many scars and cuts that I was too afraid to even look at them. I heard more giggling outside the door as I threw my dress over the door so that it was slightly hanging. I looked at the red dress. It was beautiful, but not my type.

I pulled it on anyways. It was a size too small, but I would live. It was tight on my body. Too tight. It took an extra effort for me to breathe. I hated the fact that it exposed most of my chest which had the most scars. I rubbed my arms and finally spoke, "I don't think it's the dress for me." My voice was softer than usual. I tried to pull it down lower, but it only shot right back up. I didn't hear a reply, so I opened the door. I looked around, seeing that I was alone. "G-Guys?" I whispered in fear. I closed the door to the changing room and deciding to change. They were probably waiting for me on the outside of the changing room set. I put my hand up to grab my dress, but found that it was empty. I turned around in a flash and saw it was missing. I quickly put on my flats before dashing out the room.

I bumped into a human on my way and ducked. "I'm sorry!" I cried running out the door. A loud alarm rang throughout the mall, and I turned around to see a red light flashing in the doorway of "Forever 21."

"Thief!" A man yelled pointing at me. Me? I'm no thief! I grew even more scared and I began to run towards the exit. Where was my bodyguard? I dashed out the door and looked for the limo. I found it nowhere in sight. They left me? I felt a lump form in my throat, and tears welled in my eyes.

"No! Get away from me!" I cried as someone grabbed my arm. I yanked it back and scooted away, only to fall on my rear end on the sidewalk.

"Thea, it's just me. Let's go." My bodyguard appeared. He grabbed my arm tightly and began waking towards the back of the mall. His expression was serious.

"No! I can't go back there! Please!" I begged as I saw the limo filled with the girls as they laughed at me. He ignored me and nearly threw me in with them. I was too afraid to look up.

"You should've seen your face!" Sophie laughed. Why were they so mean to me? I did nothing wrong to them. I thought they were my friends.

"Stupid girl," Emily snorted. Misty kicked my stomach hard making me gasp. Lola yanked me up by my hair and slapped me as hard as possible. I screamed, but the limo was soundproof. She ripped off the dress with her hands and threw the servant dress at me. "You're nothing. You will never be special. You're just an omega. A maid. You're worthless!" Emily spat on me as I scrambled up. I didn't cry. I forced my tears to stay inside. I didn't want them to know it affected like it did. I pulled on the dress and crawled into the corner of the limo. I just wished it would all just go away.

But like usual, my wishes never came true.

•••

I shut the door as soon as I was back in my room, and I locked it. "What happened?" Josh dropped a box he was holding and rushed to me. I blinked multiple times to keep my tears from escaping, but that only made it worse. The tears rolled down my cheeks as Josh assessed me. He brushed lightly over the place where I had been slapped. "What did they do?" He nearly whispered looking at me in the eye.

I ignored him and began to pull off my dress. When it fell to the ground, I couldn't hold back my sobs. Bruises, and new cuts formed on my body. "Thea...." Josh traced over each one with the tip of his finger. I had no words. No words to explain what pain I had experienced. Suddenly, he became angry and turned away. "Why the hell did they do that?" He growled with his back facing me.

"I-I.... I don't... kn-know!" I covered my body with my arms and Josh sagged his shoulders.

He lowly replied, "If only I'd been there. I see.... I'm seeing a 16 year old kid being abused, and I can't do anything about it!" He turned around and faced me quickly. "This isn't okay. They aren't your pack, Thea. They don't love you!" He shouted. I couldn't reply because I was drowning myself in the sound of my sobs. His eyes softened and he embraced me, "I'm sorry," was the only thing he said. "So so so so sorry." I only held him tighter. "Why don't we get your mind off of it?" He asked softly as he picked up my dress and slowly put it back on me.

I held out my hands for him as he pulled it back down and nodded. "I was going through some stuff while you were gone." He lifted the box he was holding earlier and I looked at the label. Her beautiful handwriting said: Memories. Scrawled in cursive at the top. It was mama's box. I had seen her look inside it a few times and even cry a little. I was too scared to even look to see what it was. "Only if you want to, I mean, I think it would look good on you," he stammered nervously.

What does he mean it would look good on me? "May I see?" I wiped the rest of my tears as he opened the box and I crawled over to it. I lifted the beautiful green gown and my eyes grew a fraction of a bit. It was a dress. Mama cried over a piece of clothing? How odd? Unless it was real sentimental to her. Maybe I shouldn't be wearing it at all.

It was a floor length dress that was the same color as Mama's eyes. I could easily tell it was a dress of her own making by the stitches she used whenever she fixed holes in my dress. There was a thin layer of green see-through fabric as the straps with small sparkles on it. The first half of the dress that covered until the lower region of my stomach was lightly sparkled and looked tight-fitted. The rest of the lower dress flowed down freely. It was the perfect gown. More than I could ask for. "I don't know... It's her dress. Mama's dress." I whispered dropping it back into the box.

Josh pulled away the box before the dress fell inside and it instead landed on the bed. "I'm pretty sure she would want you to wear it, Thea. Trust me on this, alright?" he placed his hand on mine and stared into my eyes. My lips parted, and I nodded quickly. She would. I knew she would.

A sudden smile overcame my face, and I dried the excess tears on my cheek. Josh grinned at me lopsidedly and I picked up the dress once again. I held it against myself and twirled in circles. I giggled as I came to a stop and watched the world move as a result of my dizziness. Josh laughed and held out his hand, "M'lady, may I have this dance?"

I took his hand and replied, "Yes you may, good sir." I replied in the best tone I could possibly muster. He began to twirl me around, and we sashayed around the room. I couldn't help but laugh the entire time.

•••

I brushed my hair throrougly to get rid of the extra knots and tangles. My hair looked different when it was straightened. It took hours to do, because I didn't have a straightener. I instead used the heat of 2 irons I managed to grab and use them on low heat to straighten my hair.

I smoothed out my dress and put on my usual flats because I had no other shoes, and Mama's dress covered my feet well. I opened the door to the bathroom and Josh looked up at me and grinned. "D-Do I look good?" I asked.

He smiled, "You look beautiful, Thea."

"Thanks Josh." I blushed as he approached me. He rubbed my cheek and I knew his thumb was over the burn mark Beta Bryce had given me a couple days ago.

He looked away towards the door, "Someone's coming." he rushed back into his room, and I quickly masked his scent with my perfume.

"Thea?" the door creaked open, and Jake peeked his head in slowly, "Are you ready?" he asked once noticing I was fully dressed.

"Yes sir." I replied looking at the ground.

"No need for formalities, remember? Especially at this ball. Just enjoy yourself while you can." he assured.

I nodded and he waved me over. No formalities. He shut the door after me and we walked down the hall. "Why are you nice to me?" I blurted out. "I mean, I'm sorry, I didn't-"

Jake shook his head, "You're a sweet girl, Thea. You just stand out from the rest." he shrugged. He put his arm in mine like Misty and Sophie had. I began to feel fear.

"No," I whispered. "No, not again." I gulped. It was another trick. He wasn't my friend, he was pretending to be. I stopped in my place.

"What's wrong?" Jake asked.

"Please. Please don't do this to me." I begged unlatching my arm from his.

"I'm your friend. You can trust me." he tried to reassure.

"No, not again. I can't-I don't want to be hurt again." I pleaded.

"Relax, okay? I'm not like the others." he grabbed a hold of my shoulders and gently shook me. I stared into his eyes. They were sincere and filled with an emotion I couldn't figure out. I slowly nodded. "I promise." he added reaching for my hand. I squeezed it and he asked, "Shall we continue?"

I nodded and whispered, "Yes." before we continued our walk towards the ball. My first ball.

•••

I took a deep breath as Jake opened the double doors. Jake squeezed my hand again reassuringly and we made our way through the crowd. The music was classical, yet at the same, it was quick. "Isn't it the talk of the town." A familiar voice called out and grabbed my shoulders. I flinched unconsciously and turned to see Alpha Xavier with another girl beside him. "Theadora, is it?" he asked smiling at me.

"Thea, yes s-" I cleared my throat, "Yes."

Alpha Xavier shook my hand, "Nice to see you again. Call me Xavier. This is my daughter Erin."

Erin smiled, "It's nice to meet you, Thea. Thank you for saving my father." she shook my hand also.

"Nice to meet you too, this ball is beautiful."

"I did help plan it all, thanks to Jake." she smiled at him with something her eyes.

Jake seemed at a loss for words and I couldn't help but giggle. 'Is it okay if I dance with Erin?' Jake's voice broke through my mind. I couldn't reply, so instead I nodded at him.

"Erin, uh, do you think we could maybe dance?" he asked.

Erin's eyes brightened, "I would be delighted." she took his hand I dropped Jake's. Xavier nodded approvingly towards Jake and the 2 scurried off on the dance floor.

"Thea, I never had the chance, but I would like to say thank you. What you did was amazing, and you will forever be in my debt. I just want you to know that there is always an available space in my pack for you if you need it. I've seen the way they treat you, and I just want to offer my help. Taken note that if you leave here, you won't be considered an omega. You will be treated as a normal pack member, I promise you that." he nodded.

"What are you 2 chatting about?" Alpha Alexander's hand was felt on my shoulder and I became stiff.

Xavier cleared his throat, "We were just finishing up. Thank you Thea, and think about it." Xavier nodded at me and walked off.

Alpha Alexander disappeared as soon as Xavier left and I was left alone in the middle of the party. I smiled at Erin and Jake laughing and dancing. They were a beautiful couple. I decided to make my leave. I didn't feel right being in the room with everyone else. I felt like an outcast. I began walking towards the hall. The music became faint and more faint.

"You! Stop!" A familiar voice shouted from behind me. I froze. "Thea? That's you?" Beta Bryce rubbed my cheek as he caught up to me. I gulped as the stench of alcohol consumed my insides.

"You're drunk," I whispered.

He narrowed his eyes, "That's sir to you." He slapped me hard making shock overcome my body as my head turned. "Funny how there's a party thrown for you just down that hall, and you're down he," he whispered rubbing my cheek where he slapped it. "You look sexy, babe." He grabbed my wrists as I stood frozen. "I never punished you for stabbing me," he added.

"N-No, please, sir." I pleaded.

"I love it when you beg," he snarled opening the door to one of the rooms. He pushed me on the bed and locked the door.

"No!" I screamed jumping off of the bed. He slammed me down on the bed and sat up on my body to anchor it. "Please!" I cried as tears fell from my eyes. He unbuckled his pants as he kissed my neck. I tried to push him away but he held me down. "I'm sorry." I cried as he pulled down his underwear and slammed himself inside my body. I gasped and screamed in pain.

He put his hand on my mouth and continuously rammed as hard as he could inside of me. I cried helplessly. I couldn't do anything.

I was being raped by my beta, and I couldn't do anything about it.

•*Chapter 8*•

Theadora Sanford•

I softly cried as I held onto the broken pieces of green fabric that was left. It was ruined. Her dress was ruined. I stared at Beta Bryce's sleeping figure on the bed. He did this. He raped me, and destroyed mama's dress. What did I do to deserve this? I made sure my sobs were at a low level so that no one would hear me, and I would be punished for waking anyone up. I gathered as much of the fabric as I could and slowly opened the door to the room. Beta Bryce was a monster.

I ran as fast as I could downstairs. I slowed as I came to the basement and stared at the door at the end of the hall. I began to walk then. I was holding the fabric against my chest as tears fell down my cheeks. I was tired of crying and feeling sorry for myself. I wanted to do something, but, I couldn't. No one would understand what I went through everyday. Not even Josh.

As I opened then door to my room, I relaxed when I heard Josh's snores. I didn't want to wake him and have him worry about me. I gently placed the broken fabric in it's original place in the box and walked into the bathroom. I stared at my body in horror. Hickeys surrounded my neck area, and my eyes were bloodshot. My skin was a sickly pale and my hair was no longer straight and fancy. It was messy and out of place. Like me.

I hugged myself and put on a brand new pair of undergarments. I put on my night gown afterwards and stared at my exposed neck. I couldn't stand staring at the things Beta Bryce caused. When I opened the door, I was shocked to see Josh standing in the doorway without a shirt on. "Thea? What took you so long?" he yawned stretching. "What time is it?" I didn't reply as he looked over me. I looked down and used my hair as a curtain for my neck.

"I don't know." I managed to whisper without a single sob.

"What's wrong?" He sounded worried and lifted my head, "Why were you crying?" He asked. I tried to swallow the hole forming inside throat. He looked over me before his eyes became hard and his eyes grew darker. "Who did this?" He demanded pulling back my hair and looking my neck. "Dammit, Thea. Who?"

I flinched as he raised his voice and replied, "B-Beta B-Bryce."

Josh began to shake, "What did he do to you?" He growled. I stayed silent. "Thea, what did he do?" He demanded angrily.

I couldn't take it anymore. I screamed, "He raped me, Josh! He raped me!" my eyes began to water again, and Josh looked on the verge of shifting.

"Thea," Josh began, "you can't stay here. You.... You can't!" He growled.

"No! I can't go!" I cried. "Don't make me leave!"

"When were you going to tell me he raped you?" Josh demanded. "When!" He repeated.

"I-I wasn't going to," I whispered bowing my head.

"Why? I need to know this stuff!" He shouted making me flinch. I was afraid he would hit me.

"I-I'm sorry. P-Please don't hit me." I begged holding up my hands to cover my face.

The atmosphere seemed to grow lighter and his anger diminished within the second. "I won't hurt you. I can't hurt you. Damn, I'm sorry for yelling I should've..." he covered his face. "I'm sorry," he finally sighed.

I hugged him tightly, "It's okay," I mumbled onto him. He rubbed my hair and stared at me.

"You're so... Innocent," he managed.

I tilted my head, "How so?"

He shook his head, "Doesn't matter. Head off to bed."

I nodded and made my way to my bed. "Josh," I called out softly as I got in the bed. I was still surprised we hadn't woken up the entire house with our banter. "could you sleep beside me?" I asked gently. He turned off the bathroom light and his footsteps got closer and closer to me. He sat down on the small space beside me and I scooted closer to him so that there was more space. He lazily slung his arm around me. I silently said my prayers and mumbled, "Goodnight, Josh."

"Good night," he grunted.

•••

When I woke up, Josh's snores were the only sound I could hear. There was something about him holding me that made me feel warm inside. The feeling vanished when he began moving around. His eyes flew open and grew big as he looked at the clock. "Shit." he whispered getting up fast and putting on his shoes.

"Josh?" I asked as he threw on his scarf.

I wasn't sure if he ignored me, or didn't hear me. "Come on, Cat." he called. Cat's furry head appeared from his little room and began to follow Josh. I tilted my head.

"Josh? What's wrong?" I asked.

He turned to me, "You have lessons today as soon as I get back," was the only thing he said before climbing out the window with Cat. He poked in his head, "and make sure to mask my scent." he added before shutting the window and leaving me. I huffed irritatedly and got up.

I walked into the bathroom to wash up. I completed my business fast with my usual shower and whatnot and put on my usual clothing. I was somewhat sore down south, but I tried my best to ignore it. I rushed out the door and into the kitchen, only to see that breakfast was already fixed. I sighed in relief as I noticed it was only Riley. "I made breakfast for you." she smiled at me.

I nodded silently and whispered, "thank you." Riley was a decent maid. She chose to be a maid, and no one really cared. She would sometimes do chores for some of the others, but it was the first time she did them for me.

She walked passed me and left the kitchen as she finished the plates. The pack normally sat together at the dining room and had special meals cooked for professionals, but I was usually the one who made the meals if it were a normal occasion in the smaller kitchen. I wiped my hands on my dress as Beta Bryce entered. I grew nervous and afraid. Alpha Alexander followed behind him with a stern expression.

"You disappeared last night." Alpha Alexander noted without looking at me.

"Yes, sir. I grew tiresome quickly. I apologize if it came off as rude, sir."

He shook his head, "No worries, just don't do it again. You'll look like a fool to Xavier. Although, that's what you are."

I stayed silent and glanced at Beta Bryce as he ate. His face was hard and angry. Was he always that angry? He frowned too much, in my opinion. When he looked up at me, more anger flooded his sight and he threw his plate at me. I gasped as it fell to the ground and shattered just before hitting me.

•••

"Cat!" I exclaimed hugging the adorable ball of fur with legs and a tail. He purred in response and I kissed his head. "Where's Josh?" he meowed in response and rubbed his head on my leg.

"Josh?" I called out. There was no response. I looked at the open window. He was still out there. He should be back by now. That was odd. I set Cat on the floor and strained my ears just in case I was missing something.

I felt a hole inside of myself. I felt as if something was wrong out there. But I couldn't go. The world was a scary place, and I had enough fears held inside this home.

•Chapter 9•

Theadora Sanford•

"Birds flyin' high, you know how I feel.

Sun in the sky, you know how I feel.

Breeze driftin' on by, you know how I feel.

It's a new dawn, it's a new day, it's a new life for me.

Yeah, it's a new dawn, it's a new day, it's a new life for me,

ooooooooh...And I'm feelin' good."

I slowly opened my eyes and let the tunes of my alarm clock absorb my mind. It was one of my favorite songs. I closed my eyes and continued, "Fish in the sea, you know how I feel." my voice was drowsy and quiet. I slowly got out of bed, "River runnin' free, you know how I feel!"

I ran into the bathroom and began to brush my teeth while attempting to sing, "Blossom on the tree, you know how I feel.It's a new dawn, it's a new day, it's a new life for me, and I'm feelin' good!" I rinsed out my mouth and wet one of my cloths. I wiped my face clean and sang louder, " Dragonfly out in the sun, you know what I mean, don't you know, Butterflies all havin' fun, you know what I mean." I wiped on my deodorant and took off my night gown.

"Sleep in peace when day is done: that's what I mean, and this old world is a new world and a bold world for me..." I put on my dress and grabbed my hairbrush. I ran it through my tangled locks. " Stars when you shine, you know how I feel. Scent of the pine, you know how I feel!"

I began using my brush as a microphone, "Yeah, freedom is mine, and I know how I feel... It's a new dawn, it's a new day, it's a new life for me!"

I snapped my fingers, "Adooba bobba hiddledum dum a mana me mana me nee na! Hiddley hey hum! Ohhhhh yeah!" I attempted to imitate her scat.

"And I'm feelin'... gooooood." I ended on a strong note as I put on my flats and stopped my alarm clock before it could play the song again.

Cat was watching me closely on my bed. He loved it when I sang. He began to purr and meow as if applauding me. "Thank you, good sir." I giggled taking a bow for him. I hopped on the bed and he crawled on my stomach. He began to lick my cheek making me laugh. "Cat, I have to go work." I told him and he stopped licking my face. He meowed and hopped back down from my bed.

Something occurred to me, and I instantly ran to Cat/Josh's room. It was empty. Uh oh. Where was Josh? I began to grow worried. What if something bad happened to him? The worst things I could possibly imagine filled my brain and I was scared. Josh was okay. Don't worry about him. He's going to come back..... Right? Even if he doesn't, so what? You don't have real friends, Thea. It's just acting. I closed my eyes and just accepted it. I grew attached to people quick. Maybe because of my lack of relationships with anyone. The last person I could trust was Mama, and she left me, too. It was only a matter of time before Josh did as well.

I closed my eyes. Cat's low meow was my reminder of my work. I got out of bed and dashed down the hallway. Riley and I switched duties for a while. I would be doing laundry, and pool duty. I didn't understand the pool duty. In fact, I had no idea what a pool was. I decided to get laundry duty over with, because it was morning and everyone was usually too drowsy to even be upset, and I heard that the laundry room hardly had anyone there most of the time. I gathered all the clothes and ventured to the laundry room. My stomach was growling as I separated the clothes in lights, darks, colors, and other. The loads were small since there was a laundry collection no less than 3 days ago.

"Haven't you heard?" Mabel, one of the owners of the laundromat questioned another worker, April.

"Heard...?" April dragged.

"Future Alpha Jake is searching for our Future Luna."

"Anyone in particular you've seen him with?"

I automatically strained my ears to hear their conversation. "I believe it to be Alpha Xavier's daughter, Erin. Or, maybe..." Mabel searched the room and spotted me. I looked away and turned on the machines as they roared to life and began to wash the clothes. "Ahem," she smoothed out her dress. Mabel leaned down and whispered in April's ear, "The pack whore." it took a lot to be able to hear her. I had to become really silent because I didn't have the enhanced werewolf abilities like the others due to the fact that I lost connection to my wolf.

April's eyes shot up to mine, but I pretend like I didn't hear or see anything. Everyone knew I was mute around others. I only spoke to my superiors only because I was forced, and some servants from time to time. Besides that, no one really cared about me or anything I had to say.

I closed my eyes and rushed out of the room. I was glad I didn't have to return until an hour or so to put the clothes in the dryer. I decided to begin my pool cleaning to pass time by instead of being in my room.

I had to walk all the way to the back door of the pack house in order to reach the pool. It was a part of the house I'd never seen. It was one of the small meal kitchens for normal days. The door to the pool was a sliding screen. It took me a while to get it open it. I had never used such technology before. I stared at the big ovular-shaped... Well, pool. There was a smaller part with steam coming from it on the other side. I tilted my head. What contraption is this?

2 girls with towels wrapped around themselves and bathing suits walked right past me. Why were they wet? I slowly crept to the "pool." was it dangerous? It looked like a layer of glass. Maybe so. Yet, it was moving and it looked almost like water. I put my finger to it. Indeed, it was water.

I looked around to see if anyone was watching. What was the point of having a big hole filled with water? How was I to clean the pool anyway? I bent down and stared at my reflection on the water. It looked clean enough to me.

I felt something strong against my back, and before I knew it, I was tumbling into the water. My first instinct was to scream, so right before I hit the water, a strangled cry escaped my lips. I continued screaming even as I was inside the water. I didn't know what to do, or how to get out. I was gently floating to the ground. I kicked my legs and hands, trying to grasp onto anything but it didn't help. Water began to fill my lungs the more I struggled.

Is this it? Is this death? Funny thing, I didn't know water could kill. Then again, anything could.

I saw a figure in the water coming towards me. I struggled more as the person grabbed onto my waist and held me tightly. I kicked and screamed, but the person wouldn't let go. Suddenly, I felt as if I were floating. I began to rise towards the surface. Just as I broke free, everything became blurry and my eyes began to sting. I was placed on a solid ground and I felt my chest pump up and down a number of times. Coldness took over my lips afterwards, then the pumping would begin once again the same amount of times, then the air being blown into me.

I sat up as I felt the urge to puke, and I spat out water. I coughed it all out as the person rubbed my back. "Thea," he said once I finished. I blinked at the person until he became clear. "are you alright?"

"Jake?"

•••

I finished delivering the clothes to their rightful owners and returned back to my room. My first experience with the pool was frightening. Jake made sure I was okay after saving me and let me finish working as long as he had an eye on me. At least I learned how to clean a pool. Too bad I didn't learn how to "swim"- as they call it.

I folded the last shirt for the 10th floor of the pack house and put it with the other shirts on the tenth floor. It was past 8:00 which meant that clothes that hadn't been delivered were to be delivered in the morning. The other maids would take care of it in the morning. I checked the shirt's tag just to make sure none of them was incorrect. Each clothing had the floor number and room number either stamped or written on the tag so that the maids knew where to deliver them whenever we finished cleaning.

I stretched my arms and back and decided to head off. I finished all of my chores for the day. I began my journey downstairs when a really awful scent filled my nose. I nearly choked as I covered my nose. The smell was familiar, but putrid. I opened the door to my room and the scent hit me full force. I looked over at the lump in Cat's room. Cat ran up to me and then to the window. He needed air just like I did. I opened it for him and let him out before I walked back to Cat's small room. I pulled back the curtain and gasped.

It was Josh! But he was covered in blood.

•Chapter 10•

Theadora Sanford•

I looked over his body. I didn't see any cuts or anything. Was it his blood? I slowly leaned in forward and brought out my hand to touch him. I didn't know if he were asleep or still awake. Just as I was about to touch him, his eyes flew open. I quickly stumbled back as his anger-filled black eyes stared deeply into mine.

"J-Josh what happened?" I whispered. He didn't reply. "Josh?" I repeated. He got up making me scoot back even more until I was out of Cat's room and my back was against my bed.

He grabbed a black bag and walked into my bathroom. I heard the shower begin to run and I slowly crept to the door. "Josh?" I repeated in a whisper.

I stood there for 15 minutes waiting. The shower stopped and I waited expectantly. The stench of blood had worn off by then, and Cat returned in the span of 10 minutes. I leant against the door as I heard shuffling. After a long while, Josh opened the door. He was wearing clothes he didn't have before. "Wh-What happened to you?" I ask blocking the door.

He groaned, "Move out of my way."

I stood my ground and replied, "Tell me." I said in a demanding tone.

"Or what?" He raised his eyebrow while crossing his arms. I became silent. I didn't know what I would do. He took my silence as an answer and lifted me off the ground with ease. I gasped as he moved me away from the doorway and put me down again.

"Josh," I grabbed his arm he turned around and looked down at me. I forced my head down.

"It doesn't matter what happened. I'm here, aren't I?" He huskily spoke.

"Yes, but..." I looked up at him, his crystal blue eyes boring into my own. I watched him tilt his head a little, slowly pulling his head towards mine. I did the same, unsure of what was to come until we actually kissed.

I couldn't hold back anymore, I let him kiss me, and I kissed back. I could feel his lips against mine. It was a feeling of happiness which was something I had faked for 9 years. Josh pulled back in a way that made me feel lonely. He looked away from me, his eyes finding the ground. "I-I can't... We can't."

I gulped, hating the feeling of rejection, although it has been there my entire life. "Why not?" I dejectedly questioned.

"Because, you're... You're still a kid, Thea. I'm 18 years old, turning 19 in a matter of months. You're 16 and.... This.... This isn't- it won't work out."

I put my hand over his, "It will. Why not?"

"You might find your mate, and with me in the way-"

Now he was just making excuses, "Josh, you know mates are rare. No one has them anymore. There's a 1 in a million chance I'll find him. Please don't leave. Our friendship means everything to me. It's all I have." I begged, feeling the tears again.

"Thea, I won't leave you. And I know our friendship is important, but it's becoming too much. I... I've grown... Close to you."

"That's what friendship is, you grow close to eachother." I whispered, just trying to find a way to cheer him up.

"No Thea, when I say I've grown close to you, I don't mean just friendship. I want to kill every single person that's laid their hands on you, I want to rip them limb from limb. I want to please you, and make you happy. I want to kiss you, and hold you.... And..... And I want to love you, Thea."

I gulped, "Then what's stopping you?"

Without delay, Josh kissed me hungrily. His canines were begging to come out. I could tell he was suppressing his wolf, but having a hard time. His eyes switching from blue to gold, it was making me dizzy. I kissed him back as he gently laid me on the bed. I couldn't get enough of him. I wanted more of him, it was killing me inside. He slipped his tongue inside of my mouth, making me moan as his tongue made friction with mine.

I had never felt the feeling before. The feeling of pleasure, it was exciting. "Josh," I moaned as his hands roamed my body, the feeling of his skin on mine made it more exciting.

His eyes became focused, he kissed my chin, and slid down to the side of my neck, his eyes were completely gold. "Say you're mine." He growled grazing his teeth along my neck. I closed my eyes, a soft moan finding it's way into the air again. He growled when I didn't respond. He flicked his tongue across my neck, sucking and kissing it.

"I'm yours," I whispered, feeling his teeth sink inside of me before I knew it. I whimpered in pain, attempting to push him off of me. "Josh." I cried out in pain, still attempting to fight him. The state he was in scared me, "Josh, you're hurting me." He snapped out of his daze, his eyes returning to their normal blue as his canines retracted and he pulled away, his eyes searching mine.

"I'm so sorry, Thea. I... I don't know what got into me. My wolf... He... He thinks you're someone. I'm sorry."

"Wh-Why did you bite me?" I cupped the part of my neck where he bit me, but Josh brushed my hand away, examining it.

"My wolf wanted to mark you, but it's not deep enough. It'll be gone by the hour. I'm sorry." He repeated his apology.

"It's okay," I whispered. "Wh-What's a mark?" I questioned. I knew the word, but it was so faint.

"It's when a male wolf claims his..."

I stared at him in wonder, "His what?"

"Mate." Josh forced out, a frown on his lips.

I put the puzzle pieces together myself, "Your wolf thinks I'm his mate. Why?"

"I don't know," he sighed. "He won't stop talking about you, asking about you, wanting to mark you and mate with you. I don't know..." He bit his lower lip, analyzing my reaction.

My wolf was howling in the back of my mind for some reason, I couldn't really hear her, though. She hadn't spoken to me since I shifted when I was 13. I don't remember her voice, or basically anything about her, just that her name was Esmeralda. I almost felt more connected to Josh after he bit me. It was weird, something I hadn't experienced before. "Josh... What does a mark do?"

"It does alot. Claims someone, makes a stronger bond, allows a stronger mindlink, and sometimes.... Heat."

I gulped, "H-Heat?"

"Don't worry about that, my wolf didn't fully mark you, so you'll only feel a stronger bond between us, but it will go away." A small frown overcame my face. I didn't want the bond to weaken. I liked it. "You should get some rest." He sighed. "When you wake up, I'll give you the lesson I was supposed to teach today." He got off of my bed, but I grabbed his arm.

"Wait," I wasn't sure if it was because of our bond, or just me. "Can you please stay with me?"

He sighed, "We shouldn't be doing this."

"Please, Josh? Just this once?" I begged in a whisper. He looked hesitant at first, but slid in beside me. He pulled me close by my waist so that my back was against his chest. I felt peace wash over me as I closed my eyes, letting sleep take over.

•Josh Wiley•

I brushed her dark brown locks behind her ear as she dreamt. Holding her in my arms felt like magic, but I knew it was wrong. Even though she would most likely not have a mate, I had feelings for her. She was young, really young, and my wolf felt connected to her. And even more connected by the mark.

I stared at it intensely, there was a faint shape of a wolf, but it was going away. I could see the scar on her cheek, a frown found it's way on my face. I lightly brushed it with my thumb, mad that her own pack would do that to her. It made my blood boil, I would help Thea. If she didn't want to leave, then I would have to save her.

I kissed her warm lips, feeling calm at the contact, "I'm going to save you Thea, I promise." I whispered.

•Chapter 11•

Theadora Sanford•

"Ahhhh!" A crashing sound was heard. I instantly sat up. Josh was awake before me and he pushed me behind him while glaring at the source of the scream.

"Riley!" I gasped running out of the bed and after her. She ran away using her enhanced speed. "No, Riley! Please stop!" I begged chasing after her.

She stopped and I quickly tried to slow down, and I was able to stop just before I crashed into her. "A rogue!" she hissed.

"I know it looks bad. But-"

"You're sleeping with a rouge. How desperate can you possibly be?" She growled. I was at a loss for words. She thought I was sleeping with Josh? I knew it looked bad. She looked passed me and then glared, "It looks like he needs your company," she snarled storming off. My mouth slowly opened. I'd never seen Riley so upset over anything. Ever.

I didn't bother going after her. She was too fast, anyway. Was this it? Was it the end? Would she tell anyone? I felt a hand on my shoulder. My body reacted differently than usual to his touch. I unconsciously whirled around and hugged him tightly. He hugged back after a few seconds and I closed my eyes. I didn't want them to take Josh away from me. He was my friend. But somehow, I felt something more. After our kiss, I felt connected to him and it wasn't because of the mark.

"Josh," I whispered, "What we have is friendship. Only friendship. Right?" He didn't reply immediately which made me worried.

"Let's go, Thea. You need to get to work," he replied avoiding my question completely. I bit my cheek and we both walked back into the room and avoided the broken plate on the ground. Riley was only bringing me food and she saw Josh. I searched my drawer for a clean dress. Once I discovered one, I pulled it out along with other necessities as Josh opened the window. He let Cat out first before himself.

"You know what to do," he sighed as he stared at me.

I nodded, "Yes si-I mean, yes."

"Thea..." he began. I looked up at him expectantly. After a few more seconds he shook his head and mumbled, "nevermind," and shut the window.

I shook it off and sprayed the perfume all over my room before going into the bathroom.

•••

I didn't see Alpha Alexander or Beta Bryce at the breakfast table. It was only Future Alpha Jake, and Luna Erica. I was afraid Riley was going to tell someone about Josh. I needed to get access to her, but she wasn't an assigned maid like the rest of us. She chose to do it.

"The breakfast was delicious, Thea." Jake washed his plate even though he didn't have to.

"Thank you, sir." I bowed.

"Remember what I said about formalities?" He chuckled.

"Sir, but when there are other superiors in the room-"

"Nonsense, I'm going to be the superior soon enough." He snapped.

I didn't reply because I could feel Luna Erica's glare at me.

I only nodded and turned around to walk away. I didn't want to go against Future Alpha Jake's wishes, but neither did I to Luna Erica. I decided to stay more vigilante throughout. With me harboring a rogue. I would surely, without a doubt, be given a death sentence. Sure, death was the easy way out, but I was never going to let them win.

•Josh Wiley•

There was something about the pack that was really off. I'd been observing them from far away. But it was mostly the alpha and beta of the pack. They all had the same cold, dead look in their eye. Their wolf seemed to be in control of their emotions most of the time.

I didn't see why Thea couldn't just leave. It would be easy, especially with me here. I knew survival, and I didn't want to leave without her. At the same time, I had feelings for her I shouldn't have had.

After my wolf and I found out she'd been raped he completely took control and went on a rampage. He killed a few wolves, but mostly besides that it were just innocent animals like deer and bunnies. He was wrong for what he did, and he knew it. Those helpless animals were just like Thea. They both needed some sense of protection. I wasn't going to lie, Thea's title wasn't what made her weak, it was her that made herself weak. She let herself fall victim to those ruthless wolves. She didn't know what they'd done, and I wasn't going to be the one to tell her, either.

I remembered the look in Alexander's eyes the day he killed off both of my parents. He swept my entire pack out. The only ones he left were the kids. The helpless, weak kids. We didn't know what to do or where to go. Everywhere we went, eventually one kid either ran away, went missing, or was killed. Soon enough, I became a lone wolf after a rouge attack. I spent years in a human family until I was 15, and ran away with Marshall, Kara, and the others.

'Do you hear that?' my wolf asked. I froze as Instructed my ears to hear even the slightest fall of a leaf. Snap!
I quickly turned around to face whoever it was. To my surprise, no one was there. I pretended to lay it off and I decided it was too

dangerous to be out right now. I stretched my back and took off in a leap.

•Theadora Sanford•

I slowly opened the door to the room. I expected someone to jump out and scream, "what are you doing?" but that wasn't the case. The room was still filthy which meant Riley hadn't gotten to it yet. I figured out soon enough she was helping another maid clean the 6th floor bedrooms. I just needed to explain myself to her, and I would be done.

"Um, what are you doing?" I nearly jumped out of my skin as I turned around and faced another maid.

"Oh, me? I'm just... Uh..." I racked my brain on excuses but came up with nothing.

"I'll take it from here." Riley appeared from behind her. "Go on ahead." she smiled warmly at the other maid who gave another glance before walking off.

"Riley! I've been trying to reach you for a long while. Look, I just want to say-"

"You slept with a rogue." she finished off for me.

"No! No! I never slept with him in that way. I found him the other day and I was helping him back to health. He's helping me, really. He's no threat to the pack, I promise you."

"Honestly Thea, I don't care. Do whatever you like. And if he does cause trouble, I'm not snitching on you. I'm not a tattle tale. He's your problem, and not mine. I'm not going to barge in your business."

I didn't know what to say. "Thank you!" I closed my eyes, "Thank you so much. I hope we can still be friends."

"Of course we can. I gotta head off. I'll see you around, yeah?"

"Oh, uh, yes, yes you will." she walked passed me and I let out a breath of relief. All that worrying for nothing. I sighed and stared at her back as she walked into one of the bedrooms with her cleaning supplements.

When making sure the coast was clear, I snuck on the elevator. I wasn't allowed on the 6th floor unless it was my laundry day. If I were caught, God knows what would happen to me.

As the elevator opened, my eyes grew big at the sight of Alpha Alexander. I gave a polite bow, "A-Alpha...." I began to stutter making me scared. Don't stutter.

"What are you doing on the elevator?" he demanded. His cold, black eyes catching mine as I looked up by accident. I looked away as fast as possible. "You travel by foot. You have no reason to slack off and use an elevator." he snarled.

"Yes sir." I whispered.

"I can't here that. Speak up."

"Y-Yes sir." my air restriction was cut off as Alpha Alexander held my throat in a tight grip and slammed me against the wall.

"I said do you understand!" he shouted.

"Yes sir. I understand!" I gasped out. He let go of me and stepped onto the elevator as if nothing happened.

"Get the hell out of my sight." he snarled lastly. I didn't waste a second dashing out of the room.

I took in deep breaths as I safely made it to the basement door. When I opened the door, I quickly shut it at the sight of Cat trying to get out. "No, boy." I said walking into the bathroom. Cat followed whilst softly meowing. I examined my neck. He didn't squeeze it enough for a bruise to form, that was good.

I sighed in relief and Cat began rubbing my leg aggressively. "Yeah, boy?" I asked. He ran out of the bathroom and began rubbing his front paw on the door. "No, Cat." I lifted him but he began moving around wildly.

"Cat, you already ate lunch, didn't you?" I looked in his room to see his bowl empty. I sighed and put him down. What has gotten into that cat?

The window opened and I smiled warmly at Josh, "Ready for lessons?" he asked shutting the window and putting his shoes in his bag. He pulled out a pencil and paper and sat down on my bed. That was fast preparation.

I nodded, "Yes sir. I mean, yeah." I blushed.

•*Chapter 12*•

Theadora Sanford•

"The cat and dog were excited about playing their-" I stopped at the word. "their ex lo- no..." I stopped as I tried to pronounce the word. "Exlopuhone?" I stared at the word in confusion. "I'm so stupid," I mumbled pushing the book away.

"No you're not. You're just learning. Do you need help with it?" I hated when I needed help. I nodded either way. "Xylophone. Ziy-lo-phone," he sounded out.

"Xy-lo-phone." I repeated.

"Go ahead and rest. We'll continue tomorrow." He closed the book and I sat up in my bed and stared at Josh.

"Josh... You know you've healed completely," I began.

"Yeah?"

"And... And you haven't left." He raised his eyebrows.

"Because... I'm teaching you how to read," he explained.

"That's it?" I whispered expecting more. After our kiss... And every-thing? That was all. I felt broken inside.

"Thea, don't take this out of proportion, what we have-"

"No. Just.... Just Don't. Please.... Friendship. This is strictly friend-ship."

"Thea-"

"So you kissed me because that's what friends do?" I cut him off.

"I can't control my actions sometimes, I'm sorry."

"No, I'm sorry." I just wanted the conversation to end. "I just need to ask you one more thing."

"Shoot."

"Why are you so nice to me?"

Josh sighed, "Because," he stood up, "I've been through the same thing."

"It still isn't fair you have to do this. You can leave anytime you want, you know? It just causes more trouble for you if you stay. I'm fine right here."

Josh's eyes met mine in an instant, "No," he stated.

"No?"

"No. You aren't fine, you will never be fine, Thea. You live... You live..."

"It's been this way my entire life. I really am okay."

"I can see it in your eyes. The pain, the fear, the sadness. You aren't fooling me." Josh moved closer to me. His eyes were squinted, "Don't ever tell me you're okay. I will never believe you are okay unless you are rid of.... Of.... This." I stared at him as his anger was replaced with relief. His expression became calm and he kissed my forehead softly. "Goodnight, Thea," he mumbled before walking back into the smaller room. I brought my knees up to myself and did the one thing mama told me to do in a time of need.

I prayed.

•••

'Birds flyin' high, you know how I feel-' I quickly pressed my alarm to snooze before the music could continue. I rubbed my eyes and glanced around the room. Josh was putting on his shoes.

"Morning." he nodded towards me.

"Good morning." I yawned. He smirked at me before opening the window and disappearing into the snow. He shut it afterwards and I looked around for Cat. Josh must have already let him out.

The door to my room opened and I gasped as Riley ran up to me. "They're checking inventory and word out is their looking for a runway rogue," she informed.

My eyes grew big as I grabbed my perfume and sprayed it all around my room. "Where is he?" Riley asked pulling back the small hand-made curtain and seeing that it was empty besides 2 cups which were Cat's food and water bowls.

"He went out." I quickly put on my normal work dress and flats before I glanced at my room once more.

"Come." Riley ushered me speedily into the first floor for the privileged maids. Every single one was lined up against the wall. Riley and I followed their lead and stood beside the rest. Guards were throwing everything in each room by flipping bed and smashing things.

I closed my eyes and took in deep breaths to calm my rapid heart. If they knew I was nervous, they'd definitely flip my room upside down just for a speck of evidence of Josh's existence.

I began to mumble my prayers to relax myself. It worked to my luck and as soon as every room was inspected, they headed downstairs towards my room. Riley worriedly glanced at me as I continued to mutter my prayers under my breath. "Our father, who are in heaven, hallowed be thy name. By kingdom come, thy will be done on earth as it is in heaven. Till' this day-"

"All clear." A deep voice barked making everyone, including me, relax. The guards turned the opposite way and marched up the steps.

"Close one." Riley exhaled, "You're welcome, by the way." She added giving me a small grin.

"Oh, yes! Thank you. I have to head off to go cook breakfast. Sorry to leave so quickly." I tried my best to excuse myself politely.

"I get it, go on," she laughed a little. I sighed and headed towards the kitchen.

Alpha Alexander, Future Alpha Jake, and Beta Bryce weren't at the breakfast table. It was just a couple of pack members whom I couldn't name and Luna Erica. "What're you making?" Luna Erica demanded as soon as she entered.

"Eggs, bacon, and pancakes, Luna." I bowed my head before her.

I heard her gag, "No, no. I'm on a diet. I need something more healthy," she explained walking past me and searching the cabinet. "When did it last eat?" Erica asked as she sensed Alpha Alexander's presence in the room. I kept my head down as Alpha Alexander hugged his mate and kissed her cheek. His dark eyes settled on her. I looked away before he caught my eyes and put my attention back on the floor.

"When did you last eat, girl?" Alpha Alexander demanded.

I didn't want him to know about the McDonald's I had with Josh last night. That was too suspicious. "3 days ago, sir." I replied but my answer came out as a mumble.

"Speak up when you're talking to me." he growled.

"Thea, you're dismissed from your chores for today, and I expect you at the dinner table sharply at eight. Understood?" Beta Bryce cut through Alpha Alexander unexpectedly. Shock overcame Alpha's Alexander as he stared at Beta Bryce.

"Excuse me?" He snarled. "Are you trying to go on another one of your raping sprees," he snorted.

"Alex, trust me. I can handle the girl." Beta Bryce gave Alpha Alexander a determined look. "Do you understand, Omega?" He turned back to me and I looked down as fast as possible.

I cleared my throat, "Yes, Beta Bryce."

"Dismissed," he waved his hand and I scurried as fast as possible out of the breakfast room.

•••

"This is Josephine which is Jo for short, Amy, Elizabeth, Beth for short, and Margaret but Meg for short." I pointed to each character on the cover of mama's book and spoke to Josh about them. "Mama's favorite was Jo, because she had a tendency to care for others more than herself." I explained.

"Like you," he replied softly. I smiled a little. He was actually somewhat correct. I never realized it until then. "Who's your favorite?" He asked curiously.

"Hm," I thought for a moment before I pointed to one of the smaller women, "Beth is my favorite. She was committed to her family, and desired a life with her family. She didn't care to marry as much as she cared of being with her family. She gathered scarlet fever and the after-effects of the sickness killed her at the end when she was 13." I explained, growing sad at the mention of her death. I remembered Jo's reaction when she found her sister lying dead in her bed.

I sighed and placed the book aside. "You know, you should start reading that book sometime soon. It'll help you improve." He suggested as I began to play with his large fingers. It was initially a one time thing, but eventually became a habit that I sometimes didn't realize I was doing.

"Maybe so." I stood up and brushed myself off. I opened the small window opening for Cat to come in back easily.

"It's almost eight, Thea." Josh reminded.

"Oh, yes." I mumbled looking at my alarm clock. It was 7:58. I let out a deep sigh and Josh asked me what was wrong. "Nothing... I just.... I just.... I was thinking about mama the other day. She told me once that everybody has their own story. I wonder if mine has a happy ending, you know?"

Josh patted the spot beside him. I sat down and leant against his shoulder, "There's a really old story that people still tell today. It's called Cinderella. It's about this girl around your age, maybe older, with a deceased mother. Anyways, her father re-married an evil woman with 2 daughters and not much longer the dad died also, which leaves Cinderella with her evil step-mom and sisters. Anyways, they force her to work and clean around the house. So the word gets out that Prince Charming, their prince, is throwing a ball. Cinderella aspires to go, but her step-mom and sisters refuse to let her. So, the night the step-mom and step-sisters go out to the ball, Cinderella is greeted by her fairy god mother. She grants her a dress, glass slippers, and a ride to the ball that only lasts until 12, and then it'll change back into whatever it was before. So pampered Cinderella goes to the ball, and dances with Prince Charming. As cheesy as this sounds, they fall in love. Cinderella sees the time and realizes it's nearly twelve and runs away, but leaves one of her glass slippers on the stairs that

Prince Charming finds and keeps. The next morning, she sees Prince Charming at her door and he's asking for the foot of every women in the household to try so he could find his mystery girl. The step mom tries to hide Cinderella, but Prince Charming sees her and when the shoe fits her, he asks for her hand in marriage and you can pretty much figure out the rest. They live happily ever after."

"That's beautiful." I whisper.

Josh laughed, "Really? I mean, it's pretty corny. He falls in love by a dance."

"Sure, but don't poke holes in the story. At least she found true love in the end."

"You're lucky I didn't tell you the actual version of the story."

"What do you mean?"

"In the real version, the step mom cuts off her daughters' heels and toes so that they can fit in the shoe."

I gasped, "That's awful. Why would she want to do that."

He shrugged, "Evil step mom, remember? Crap! It's 8:05 you better

hurry." he glanced over at the clock with big eyes and I shot up from

my comfortable position on his shoulder.

"Oh, right! I'll be back." I ran out of the room, making sure to shut

the door and I made it to the dinner room. Beta Bryce was sitting

down at the end of the table sipping on Chardonnay. "I'm so sorry

for being late, Beta Bryce." I bowed.

He grinned, "No worries, take a seat." he gestured across from him. I

followed his instructions and sat down. "I'm glad you could join me,

Theadora." there was something about his face... A smile that scared

me. "Do you know why you're here, Thea?" he stood up and began

circling the table slowly.

"N-No sir." I coughed over my stutter. He laughed loudly and picked

up one of the knives.

"You're here so I can let you enjoy one of the best meals you've ever

had in your lifetime. Only because I feel generous." he smiled and

stopped just behind my seat. "Bring it on out for our guest." he called.

A group of maids came out with a platter covered with a golden top.

They placed it on top of the table and Beta Bryce nodded at two guards standing by the door. They moved in towards me, but kept their distance.

"Voíla!" Beta Bryce took off the top of the platter. My blood grew cold as I shot out of my seat and screamed. I was too stunned to even move or attempt to escape. There lying in a heap on top of the platter was a familiar looking cat. My cat.

•Chapter 13•

Theadora Sanford•

I screamed louder as Beta Bryce brought the platter closer to me. I couldn't help but cry, "Cat!" Beta Bryce had an amused grin on his face and he placed it on the space in front of me.

"Looks good, doesn't it?" he cackled evilly. He put his hands on my shoulders and forced me back into my seat as I cried. "Go on, pick up the fork." he urged.

My hand shook as I grabbed the fork, only to drop it because of the burning feeling though my hand. "Pick it up." Beta Bryce ordered. I sobbed as I grabbed the fork off of the floor and held it tightly, despite the pain. "All of it." he whispered in my ear as I stared at Cat. His fur was gone, and he had steam coming off of his body.

I closed my eyes and cried as I stuck the fork in his cooked body. I opened my eyes and took a piece out. The meat was perfectly cooked and came off easily on my fork. I cried and dropped the fork on the table. I couldn't eat him. I couldn't eat Cat.

Beta Bryce snapped his fingers and one of the guards approached him with a box. Beta Bryce opened it and took out brass knuckles with silver blades on the tip. I cried as he grabbed my arm and yanked me up. "I'm sorry! I'm so sorry! I can't do it! I can't-" he pulled off my dress and punched me in the gut as hard as possible. I fell to the ground at the impact. I looked down at my sizzling skin due to the silver.

"Get the hell up. When I tell you to do something, you do it!" he spat yanking me up and I cried out in pain. I held onto the fork and forced it into my mouth. I held my breath as I chewed so I wouldn't have to taste him. "Good girl," Beta Bryce was satisfied. "now finish the rest." he laughed.

The guards laughed as I struggled to get the meat from the small bones and eat them. My mouth burned from the silver, and so did my hand. It had gotten to the point I began bleeding as I finished half of him. I cried through each bite, chew, and swallow.

Why?

What did I ever do to deserve this? I asked myself. But like every single time, there was no response.

•••

I barged into my room, not caring that the door was open and instantly ran into my bathroom. I tripped and hit my head on the counter, but that didn't stop me from running to the toilet and emptying my body out. I couldn't take it. Every time I threw up, Beta Bryce would make me eat it again. I felt my hair being lifted as I let myself go. Josh's warm hand ran along my bare back as I finished and cried.

"Thea..." he whispered helping me up. I cried and hugged him tightly. "You're... You're..." he couldn't form a sentence.

"Cat is dead!" I sobbed. "They cooked him... And he made me eat him! I ate Cat!" I cried. Josh examined me closely. His eyes were filled with hate and rage.

"Don't talk about it. You need to rest right now." he replied lifting me up and carefully walking me to my bed. He placed me on the lumpy mattress and took out his black bag. There was a first aid kit bigger than my own that he took out. He put a substance on a white clothes and gently patted it on my stomach where I was punched. I bit my tongue from screaming as he worked.

"Take these." he took out 2 blue pills. He dashed into the bathroom and the sound of water running cut on for a couple of seconds before it cut off and Josh ran back to me with his hands cupped together. He put his hands up for me to drink for the pills. I put the pills in my mouth and drank the water, easily swallowing the 2 pills down. He went back to work on my stomach, and the more I tried to focus on what he was doing, the more tired I got.

Not much longer after, my body began to shut down and I had no choice but to close my eyes.

•••

My eyes snapped open at the sun's rays shining down on me. When I sat up, a sharp pain shot throughout my body. I whimpered and fell back down. "Hey, hey, relax, okay?" Josh came in from the window with a bag in his hand. He put the bags aside and I noticed the pillow on the ground beside me and the blankets sprawled like a bed below it. "You need to eat." he unwrapped a biscuit looking thing. He put it up to my lips and I took a small bite out of it. I chewed it slowly and Josh watched me closely.

"Thank you." I murmered once I swallowed. I couldn't eat more because the image of Cat was imprinted on my brain. "I'm not hungry." I added softly.

"Thea, I know you're lying." he sighed wrapping the sandwich back up.

"I can't get the image of Cat out of my head." I whispered. Josh laid down beside me and wrapped his arm around my neck.

"You don't deserve this. You're a great kid."

"They hate me for who I am." I mumbled glancing at Josh.

"They still have no right to do that to you. You know it's not your fault, right?"

I didn't reply because it was my fault. I shouldn't have let Cat in. I should never have rescued Josh. If I'm caught, I deserved everything given to me for disobeying. "It is my fault. Mama would be alive if I weren't here. I'm..... I'm a... I'm a mistake." I elaborated.

"She wouldn't want this for you, Thea. We've both lost our families. I know how you feel, trust me. I just don't want you to make the same mistake I made. I gave up. I have no reason to be alive. I have no purpose."

"Yes, you do. Aren't I a reason?"

He avoided my eyes, "The only one."

"You can't just think that!" I cried frustratedly.

"Do you see my point now? You shouldn't be okay with any of this."

The way he spoke and the look in his eyes made me want to believe him. I felt like he finally made his point come across and I became silent. "Maybe so...." I sighed laying back down as the door opened slightly. Josh didn't even flinch or even attempt to hide. I looked over to see Riley standing in the doorway.

She smiled at me and glided over. "Are you feeling any better?" She asked.

I smiled, "Yes, thank you. They should heal within the hour I believe." Riley nodded and Josh seemed surprised for some reason. He didn't say anything though, and I decided not to question him.

"Thea, your birthday is in 2 weeks, right?" She questioned smiling at me.

"How did you know?" I tilted my head questioningly.

"I've known you longer than you think." Her eyes became more sad than usual. I didn't remember her. Not even as a child. She shook her head and looked up at Josh, "I have to complete my chores for the day. I'll come back around dawn." Riley kissed my forehead, "Bye Thea, bye Josh." She waved at us before leaving and closing the door quietly.

•Riley Falin• 17 years ago

"Mommy!" I screamed frustratedly. She was finally letting me see my cousin for the first time. "Is this her?" I excitedly ran to the pink bundle but she stopped me beforehand making me even more upset.

"Riley," she reprimanded, "she's a newborn, so you can't be rough with her. Do you understand?"

I looked over at the bundle and nodded, "Yes ma'am."

She nodded for me to go and I looked over at her. She was the most beautiful baby I had ever seen. She was laughing and moving her fists all about. "Hi, Thea!" I smiled at her. "I'm your cousin Riley, and we're going to be best friends! We can play barbies and braid each others hair, and I can protect you from monsters!" I babbled. She only stared and smiled. ".... And we can share clothes!" Aunt Verana barged into the room in a panic.

She ran to Thea and sighed in relief when she noticed she was still there. "Vera, what's wrong?" mommy asked her.

Aunt Verana lifted Thea carefully and began to rock the laughing baby. "Shhhhhh," she murmured.

"Vera, what's happening?"

Aunt Verana began to cry, "He wants to see her," she whispered and mommy's face darkened.

"But... But I didn't know. Isn't he just visiting the pack? He should be gone by now!"

Aunt Verana shook her head, "No. H-He's back. I tried to tell Alpha, but he doesn't understand."

"Come on," mommy held onto Aunt Verana's hand, "Nothing will happen to you or my niece, I swear. It's my job as your older sister to protect you and that includes your children." She picked up Thea and placed the smiling baby in my arms.

"Zella, you can't go out there. You haven't seen him."

Mommy ignored her and bent down, "Riley, remember you and Thea are cousins. Thea is a special baby, so you have to accept that she will be different from all the others. I love you." She kissed my forehead.

I nodded and cradled Thea to me. "Zel, don't do this." Aunt Verana cried running after mommy out the door. Thea became quiet, so I made faces because she was frowning.

I could only think about what mommy said. That she was a special baby. I looked up at the door, sensing another presence. There was a boy not much younger than 1. His shining gray eyes were distant, and he didn't dare move. His eyes were attached to Thea, and just like that, he was gone.

That was the last time I saw the boy.

And that last time I saw mommy.

•Chapter 14•

Theadora Sanford•

"I'm so sorry, Cat." I bent down and placed the flower on his grave. I made the gravestone myself out of paper mache, and put his grave beside Mama's. I didn't have a body to bury, so I just gathered his belongings in a blanket and Josh dug for me.

"It's going to be okay." Josh placed his hand on my shoulder as a tear slipped out of my eyes. "I promise this won't be your forever." he added.

"Josh..." I whispered without looking at him.

"Hm?"

"Remember the story you told me? About Cinderella?" I questioned.

"Yes." he responded.

I looked up at his eyes, "Can you be my Prince Charming?"

He held my gaze. He didn't respond for a few moments. I looked back down at the snow and another tear fell. Josh's hand tilted my head upwards. "Yes," my heart skipped a beat, "but I can't promise you this is a fairytale with a happy ending."

Any ending was happy with Josh involved. At least, in my book it was. He kissed my cheek softly, "Let's get going." he whispered in my ear. I silently crouched down and opened the window. I made it inside stealthily and Josh followed behind me.

"Do you think Cat is an angel now, like mama?" I asked Josh. I sucked in a breath and tried not to cry. "I miss him." I whispered.

"Hey, hey, don't cry Thea. Of course he's an angel." he assured hugging me. "Your mom is, too. She's watching over you and she's so proud at how you've grown. Strong, smart, independent, beautiful ...." he trailed off.

"Why did people give up on the Moon Goddess?" I whispered. The Dilemma was a time when everyone stopped believing in the Moon

Goddess and a mass amount of people stopped getting mates and now having a mate is a once in a lifetime chance.

"People gave up on her because loving another person is weak." his eyes were suddenly cold and somehow he looked different.

"Does that make me weak?"

He blinked and stared at me. "Thea, wh-what?" he seemed puzzled by my question.

"I-I love y-"

He looked away, "No. Don't say it, Thea." he cut me off. "No you don't."

"B-But I thought..."

"You thought wrong. This isn't right, and you know it. Why? Just.... Why?"

"You make me feel things I've never felt before. That's why I love you." I wanted him to understand. How could he not? He kissed me!

"Stop!" he growled making me stumble away from him. Josh's nails became claws and his teeth became fangs. I threw myself towards him, "Stay back." he grumbled pushing me on the floor and my eyes shut closed as the sound of bones popping filled my ears.

Make it stop! Make it stop! Make it stop! I repeated over and over to myself. I froze when air blew against my face. I slowly opened my eyes. On cue, a scream flew passed my lips at the large beast towering above me. He growled back angrily. His eyes were completely black. The door to my room flew open, and I closed my eyes tightly. Josh grabbed his bag in between his teeth and crashed out of the window. I covered myself just in case the shards of glass cut me.

"What the hell! Are you okay, Thea?" I was frozen, but shaking on the floor. Jake placed his hand on my back and I stared up at him, "He.... He... He..." I could hardly speak. He silently grabbed my hand and lifted me from the ground.

"Don't talk, alright?" he advised helping me to my bed. "I'll tell Alpha Alexander immediately. You just stay here and-"

"No! No! Please don't tell Alpha Alexander. Please!" I begged. "You can't tell anyone!"

"Thea, don't you understand? You were attacked by a rouge! How did he get in here in the first place? Wait- Isn't that the rouge that was supposed to be killed or something?"

"Jake, please! I'm begging you." I cried. "I'll do anything!"

Jake sighed and looked at me, "Will you stop crying if I don't?"

"Yes! I promise!" I sniffed.

"Then I believe we have a deal."

•Bryce Jole•

"Oh yeah." I restrained myself from touching her just yet. She bent down low and swung herself around and unzipped my pants. "Good girl." I smirked as she grabbed my raging cock and began to suck on it. I moaned in satisfaction and the sound of my phone ringing pulled me out of my session. "Keep going." I told her as I answered the call. "What?" I growled into the phone.

"Bryce, I don't understand where I'm supposed to import the wolfsbane. They check inventory everyday." Rafael said.

I massaged my temple, "Are you deaf? I said give me the wolfsbane and I'll finish off the Jake guy, alright? Meet me tonight by the pier and we'll make the trade-off then."

"Yes sir, I'll be there at 9."

"Good." I ended the call and threw my phone back on my desk. I pushed her head down until she reached the end and began to choke. "Go all the way down. Don't half-ass it." I growled.

I leant my head back and closed my eyes. That Jake guy was going down. No one would ever take my place as alpha, and with Jake out of the way, there was no way Alexander could stop me.

There was no way anyone could stop me.

•Theadora Sanford•

I tossed and turned in my bed. I was freezing from the broken window, so I was stuck in the cold. My teeth chattered as I stared at the empty room where Josh was supposed to be.

He still hadn't returned after he shifted. Maybe he wouldn't ever come back. I didn't want him to leave. I couldn't take it. It felt different to have him so distant and I didn't know if he were coming back or not.

I didn't realize I was crying until a breeze blew in and nearly froze a tear on my face. "Please. P-lease c-come b-back." I whispered closing my eyes just as a shadow appeared in my room. I opened my eyes again and stared at the figure. It grew bigger and bigger and I had a feeling it was after me.

Something dropped inside my room from the window, and I stared at the heap on the ground. I put my blankets up as a shield as the heap stood up and formed into a man.

Josh.

I grew even more scared as he stared at me. "Thea," he rushed to me and embraced me tightly. He stared into my eyes and I felt as if he could see my soul. Without another hesitation, he brought his lips on mine in a kiss.

•*Chapter 15*•

Theadora Sanford•

I kissed back quickly. I wanted to savor every moment of his lips on mine. He swept his tongue inside my mouth and a soft moan made it's way out of my mouth.

He crawled on top of me and kissed my jaw. "Thea..." he trailed off as he kissed my neck. "I don't want anyone to touch you ever again." he grumbled, "I don't want any other man to put his hands on you ever again." He bit into my neck and I dug my nails into his bare back. I unexpectedly moaned. The pain was something I wanted to feel over and over again.

He pulled my dress above me and stared at all of my scars. I bit my cheek and quickly covered my stomach. "No," he whispered removing my hands and continued to stare making me grow frightened. He quickly leant down and kissed one. "Do you know what people say about scars?" He whispered kissing another one. He leant up and softly kissed me.

"No," I said.

"That they're tattoos with a better story." He traced one with his finger and took off my bra. He kissed one of my breasts and I bit my tongue. "You're so beautiful," he mumbled licking it. "I want you all for myself." he planted another kiss on my opposite breast.

I closed my eyes tightly and a tear slipped, "P-Please don't...." I whispered covering my body. He stopped and stared at me again. "I've felt the pain before and-"

"Thea, I promise you it won't hurt a bit," he told me softly. "and if it does, I'll stop, okay?" He grabbed my hand and squeezed it admiringly.

I hesitantly nodded and pulled my hands away from my body. This was it, wasn't it? Was this the end of my life, or just the beginning.

All I knew was that I was giving Josh me.

All of me.

He leaned down and trailed kisses down my stomach that left a searing, yet pleasureable pain. I watched as he undid his button and unzipped his pants. I squirmed around and moaned a bit. He pulled down his underwear, and I looked up, afraid I'd chicken out at any given moment.

Suddenly, I felt it. I felt him inside of me. I gasped, and my back arched upon instinct. Josh leaned over and took my hand in his as he eased in me.

"Josh," I moan. I never knew it could feel so nice. My breath hitched at his first thrust, but I groaned in pleasure once more. Josh remained silent and kissed the nape of my neck. I felt as if we were becoming one, and only he can make me feel this good.

He grunted the faster his strokes became and eventually, the bed started to creak. The sound of it drowned by my constant moaning, until finally Josh gave one last thrust and I felt an overwhelming pleasure.

"Oh my God," I gasped as I dig my nails into his bare skin. Josh looked down at me lovingly and planted a kiss on my forehead.

"Was it nice?"

Flushed, I rapidly nodded my head and he got off of me. I felt cold without him, but he left to clean up. I wrapped the blanket around me to make up for the missing warmth, and eventually Josh emerged from the bathroom with a new pair of boxers. He lied down beside me, and I rested my head on his chest. He kissed my forehead once again and I shut my eyes. No words said can describe the happiness he brought to my life.

•••

I covered my eyes as I woke up. Josh was already dressed and he kissed my cheek, "Come on, I want to show you something." he held my hand and kissed it. I yawned and pulled the covers over my chest because of the cold.

"Okay, I'll just go take a shower and-"

"There's no time. Just get dressed."

I put on my bra and panties and slipped on my dress. "I smell like sex." I grumbled.

"We both do, but don't worry about it right now." he smiled grabbing my hand again just as I finished putting on my shoes and getting out of the window. "Do you trust me?" he asked holding out his hand. I stared outside. He was taking me there? Outside?

"I-I-" my thought process stopped. I wanted to see. A burst of curiosity flooded me and I looked back at the door. I couldn't be late for work also.

"Riley's taking care of your chores for today." he spoke as if reading my thoughts.

"Yes." I soaked in his grey eyes and he lifted me up and out onto the snow.

"This way m'lady." We trudged through the snow and he held my hand for support. I found it hard to walk through the layers of snow, but I still continued. "I want to show you a few things." He said, "Not everything in the world is meant to be feared. There's always the good things that it has to offer and you have to take risks for it. Like Cinderella went against her step mother's wishes and went to the ball even though she was told not to." He explained as we entered the woods. He turned around and gazed at me, "Are you willing to risk this moment with me?"

I slowly nodded, unable to speak. He smiled and bent down on all fours. I closed my eyes tightly as he shifted. I could here the pop of his bones and movement of his muscle.

After a minute or two, everything became silent. I felt softness rubbing against my hand and I slowly opened my eyes to see a large and furry brown wolf in front of me. He was much bigger than me, and scary looking. 'Get on my back.' he told me. I grabbed his fur and threw my leg over. I held onto him as if I were on a horse.

He took off in a leap and the trees suddenly seemed to be moving passed us. I felt as if I were going to slip off, but another part of me was too exhilarated to care if it were a dangerous situation. I began laughing as we turned in so many directions and I wondered if this was what it felt like to be a wolf.

Free.

•••

Josh stopped in front of a large house in a lonely neighborhood. He opened one of the windows and held it open with his head. 'Go on.' He mindlinked me. I climbed in and he followed after me. I stared at the place in amazement. It was beautiful. There was a raging fireplace, a couch, and TV. It was a simple living room accompanied by a kitchen.

When I turned to look at Josh, I blushed when I saw he was naked. He grabbed a pair of shorts out of the black bag that sat below the windowsill and threw them on. He then closed the window and locked it.

"This house is mine." He stated, "I couldn't go through the door because the keys were in my bag, but yeah."

"How did you get this place?" I was perplexed.

"Well, this place used to belong to my adoptive human sister but she died a couple of years ago and she left me this place. My adoptive parents pay the bills for it but I own the place, and I just fixed it up."

"You have an adoptive family?" I asked.

"Well, yeah, they're humans but they know about our kind. When I was 7 or 8 I got taken in by the authorities and I was in an orphanage for a while until they adopted me, but I ran away when I was 15 or so." He shrugged.

"Why?" I asked tracing my finger along the wallpaper.

"Doesn't matter, it's in the past. But follow me, I want to show you something." He quickly shifted the subject and I decided not to pry further. He walked upstairs and I went after him. There was another small staircase on the left that led up to a closed door with a lock on it.

He continued down the hall to the last door on the end. He slowly opened it and stepped aside for me to see. My mouth slightly dropped and I gasped, "Woah." The walls were colored a pineapple tan and a king sized bed was at the end of the wall accompanied by the door to the open bathroom and another door beside it.

"This could be ours, you know? What's mine is yours, and what's yours is ours." He kissed my hand softly. "Don't think right now. I just want to show you. I want to give you the treatment you deserve. The treatment of princess." He opened the door beside the bathroom and revealed a closet full of clothing. "I'm your Prince Charming, and you can be my Cinderella."

My heart skipped multiple beats as I stared into the closet. "Josh, I... I don't know what to say." I whispered. "No one's ever..."

"I know. That's why I'm glad to be your first."

I stared at a beautiful wool sweater that was a dark red. "We'll get to that later." He held my hand and pulled me into the bathroom. "Have you ever had a hot shower?" He asked going to the glass looking room in a rectangular shape. He opened the door and turned a knob.

"No," I replied looking around the room. There was a tub near the rectangular thing and a large sink on another wall and a toilet. Decorations and other things you would find in a bathroom were all about. Josh walked me over the rectangular box and stared at me.

He didn't say anything. He just kissed me softly because no words were needed to be spoken for me to understand. I felt electricity with his lips on mine and my stomach felt lighter and as if small creatures were inside of it. Is this what love feels like?

He pulled my dress over me and placed it on the floor. He kissed my neck and unclipped my bra. He trailed his kisses lower and lower until he reached my panties and he slid them down. I bit my lip and lifted each foot until they were on the floor. He stood back up and helped me inside the box. The water instantly hit me and I stared at the shower head in amazement.

Josh followed after me not much longer after and held my waist so that my back was touching his chest. He leant down and kissed my neck. I closed my eyes and tilted my head to give him more access.

The warm droplets pounded against my bare skin in a rage and I didn't want to leave.

Josh scrubs my body with the soap, followed by his. It's not a very long shower, and I'd enjoy staying here for at least an hour, until my skin prunes like a raisin. "Why are you in such a hurry?" I question him.

Josh lifts me up suddenly. I squeal in shock, but he crashes his lips on mine. I kiss him back roughly and the taste of his saliva mixed with the water is so satisfying for me. I wrap my legs around him, but he pushes my back against the wall. "Put them around my neck," orders Josh.

I do as I'm told, and he cups the palm of his hands under my butt to lift me up. He buries his face in my area, and I feel his tongue massage it. My breathe intensifies and I pull at his hair. "Don't stop," I beg as his he continue to flick his tongue. I don't know how he can make me feel so good inside, but I never want it to stop. my legs tighten the farther he goes, and I have a lock if his hair wrapped between my fingertips.

"Josh," I give one last cry and feel myself collapse over his weight. He kisses me repeatedly down there, then finally lifts his head with a grin.

"I love when you say my name."

•••

I slipped into the sweater and searched for a pair of pants. It was the first time I would wear something other than a dress. "How did you find my size?" I asked putting on a pair of dark skinny jeans accompanied by boots.

"I checked your sizes, if that doesn't sound creepy," he chuckled making me grow weak in my knees. I laughed and when I turned around, he wrapped a scarf around my neck and put a beanie on my head.

"Thanks," I whispered as he kissed my lips and my face grew warm.

"I don't want you to catch a cold." He laughed and I excitedly grabbed his hand after putting on gloves.

"Where are we going to go?" I questioned curiously as I pulled him downstairs. "Maybe Paris? Or New York?" I grew happy at the thought of going to the Eiffel Tower, or maybe the Statue of Liberty.

He grabbed the keys out of his bag and I ran outside. I spun in circles in the snow and let it hit my face. "It's so beautiful out here!" I told him as he closed and locked the door. "This is so cool!"

"Let's get some breakfast, first. Then the fun stuff, okay?" I grinned and nodded quickly.

He pointed to a beautiful car parked in his driveway. I stopped spinning and followed him to the convertible. "Woah," I gasped, unable to form a complete sentence.

"Sweet, isn't it?" He opened the door for me and I got in. I instinctively put on my seatbelt. Josh got in on the other side and put the key in it's ignition. The car roared to life and I stared out the window at the falling snow.

Snow. It was so pure and didn't care about the world around it to stop itself from what it was doing. Was that the cost of freedom?

•*Chapter 16*•

Theadora Sanford•

I woke up with my dress on and in my room. I felt as if the last 24 hours were a dream. Something that I wished would happen, but didn't. The only thing that made me realize it actually happened was my scarf and other closed stuffed in Josh's black bag.

A smile grew on my face as I replayed yesterday's occurrence. Josh was snoring on the floor. His hair was a mess and he was holding something in his hands. I shrugged it off and got ready for my chores.

I tightened the scarf around my neck to hide the mark Josh left. I didn't know how he feels about me covering it, but it's the safest way for me at the moment. I hum my morning song as I step into the kitchen. Luna Erica was there. She gave me a bored stare and returned to gazing down at her phone. I spotted Riley as she placed Luna Eric's meal in front of her, and I nodded graciously in her direction. Riley gave me a grin back that didn't last long, as Luna Erica began to gaze at us.

I turned around and decided to head upstairs to continue laundry. I hurried upstairs and gathered all the clothes in a single basket. "Hey, you," someone called, and my blood ran cold. I gently touched the scarf around my neck and faced the stranger. He stumbled along the walls a drunken mess.

"Yes, sir?" I hurried over and bowed my head.

"Are you one of the pack whores?" He asked. "You are quite beautiful," the stranger added.

"N-No, sir," I stuttered. He stirred a little, then straightened himself with a half-empty alcohol bottle in hand.

"Please, escort me to my room." I nodded uncomfortably.

I whispered nervously, "Wh-What number, sir?"

"The one at the end." He burped and took my hand as I walked down the hall. I was too afraid to shake him, so I continued to walk. It seemed like forever until we reached his room, and he finally released my hand. I exhaled in relief and he opened the door but remained in the doorway. He stared into my eyes.

"May I leave now, sir?" I awkwardly glanced away and down at my feet. The stranger lifted my head by my chin and leaned down and kissed me. I put an effort to push him away, but he held me in my place.

I didn't know how to react. The stranger leaded me into his room and lifted me up. Afraid, I held onto his neck and pleaded, "No, please, sir!."

"Please what?" He dropped me onto the bed, and I quickly squirmed away from him and covered myself. "What's this for?" He tugged at my scarf, but I was quick to hold it in place.

He leaned in again and put his slobbery lips on mine. He tasted very strongly of alcohol and began to tug at the straps of my dress. I pounded against him and pulled away to scream. He drowned out the sound by yanking on my head and tugging me back down on the bed. He covered my mouth and removed the scarf from around my neck. He spotted the mark on my neck.

"You have a mate?" He asked. His hand slowly lifted from my mouth, and tears began to leap out of my eyes. Suddenly, a loud bang reached my ears, followed by the stranger falling over on the floor. I hyperventilated at first glance of Riley with a desk lamp in hand. She looked panicked and stricken. She lowered the lamp and reached out a hand.

"Oh, God, Riley," I gasped.

She shook her head, "Don't worry. He's the pack drunk. He won't remember a thing." She placed the lamp back in its place and lead me out the door. I quickly turned back around to retrieve my scarf. "What's that fo-" Her eyes widened as she spotted the mark on my neck. I covered it quickly as we closed the door on our way out. "Thea, don't you know what will happen if-" She nearly exclaimed.

"Sh!" I cut her off as a few misses walked by. When they were out of range, I attempted to explain, "It just... happened. I-I-"

"Thea, you could be punished! Better yet, killed!" She whispered loudly. I ignored her with a frown on my face. I'll face any penalty given to me, as I don't regret anything that happened with Josh.

"I'll face it when it comes my way," I stated proudly. They can punish me all they want, but with Josh, I felt something I've never had.

Freedom. I was more than willing to give up my life if I can be free forever.

Riley sighed, finally giving up. I was too stubborn to let her words affect me. "Well then, you should go clean up." We stopped in front of the door leading to the servant hall; where we reside. I nodded and we parted ways.

I made it to my room in no time, and I spotted Josh munching on breakfast. I didn't recognize it, and I walked over. "What's that?" I asked.

He grumbled with his mouth full, "Sandwich. Want some?" He pointed it in my direction, and I shook my head 'no.' I didn't know if I'd be able to down anything with my encounter with the drunken man. "Why do you smell like alcohol? Did your shift end early?" I dropped my gaze to the floor. I didn't know how he'd react, and I wasn't willing to find out. "Thea..." He dragged out.

"I...I... it..."

"Thea, what the hell happened? Was it Bryce? I swear to fucking God I'll-" He stood up with a start, and I was quick to grab his arm.

"No, it wasn't Bryce! It-It was just-" He turned his head around and his eyes were dark as the night sky.

"Thea, let me go. I don't give a damn who it is at this point. I'll kill everyone is this damned pack." He yanked his arm away from me, but I stumbled over to block him from the door.

"Josh, please! Please!"

"Thea-"

"I know what you're going to say, and I know! I'm weak and I don't know how to stand up for myself."

His gaze softened, "I wouldn't ever-"

"Whether you say it or not, it's true! I wasn't raised knowing what standing up for myself means, and how can I in such an abusive place? For God's sake, I don't know how to read or write! There's no way I'll ever be who you want me to be, but they're still my pack."

Josh's figure loosened, and his frown grew. He finally sighed, "Packs protect. Packs love. Packs care, Thea. They don't care about you!" He refrained, after inspecting me and finally gave up. "I'm sorry. I don't mean to hurt you, but..." I didn't face him, and walked around him. I

sat on the edge of my bed and covered my face with my hands. "Thea,"
Josh rested on the bed beside me. He wrapped his arm around me,
and I leaned over to him. He didn't say anything more, and we both
remained silent staring at the wall ahead of us.

After a long moment, I spoke up, "I wish my mama were here."

Josh replied, "I miss my family, too."

I looked up at him and furrowed my eyebrows, "I thought you ran
away?"

He laughed sadly, "I did, but that's not the family I'm talking about."

"Your real family?" Josh was quiet, and I felt my stomach churn. He
lied down and pulled me on top of him, gazing into my eyes. They
swam with confusion, and he brushed my hair back, leaving his hand
on my cheek.

"Yes."

I gulped and looked down. "I-I'm sorry."

"You haven't done anything, Thea. They were killed."

I decided to push my luck, "killed how?"

I played with his fingers and he began, "I was 2, and I don't remember much from the day. I woke up... my mom, she was screaming." A frown etched on my face as I focus on the lines on his hand. I couldn't imagine how afraid I'd be if mama ever woke me up with such a start. "You know what? You should get some rest." He suddenly stops.

"But, Josh-"

"I don't want to talk about it."

I sat up and stared at him in amazement, "Josh-"

"Thea, stop. I don't want to talk about it!" He growled angrily. I ground my teeth and turned around. There was a silence between us, and I wished it would go away. I wished everyone would go away.

•Joshua Wiley• 17 Years Ago

A high-pitched scream pierced my ears, and I sat up with a start. I saw mom covered in blood, and I grew frightened immediately. "Mom?" I asked sitting up in my bed. I spotted dad on the floor beside her, covered in blood as well, but he wasn't moving. "Momma?"

Her head snapped in my direction, and she hurried over to lift me from my bed. "Don't worry, Josh, baby," she soothed me by rubbing the back of my head. "It's going to be okay, alright?" She placed me on the ground and kissed my forehead. "Stay here, and remain quiet." She began to usher me under the bed, and I followed her orders. I didn't know how to feel. She ran over to the door and welcomed a few people in the room. My eye was caught on one of the children that were an infant. She was bursting in tears, and I couldn't keep my eyes off of her. She was so beautiful, and it made me upset she was crying. What has her upset?

I revealed myself from under the bed and followed the baby. She smelled lovely. "May I hold her?" I questioned the mother.

She looked at me in confusion. Momma spoke up, "Josh, take her and hide under the bed. Help her stop crying if you can. She'll be okay." Momma turned to the mother who nodded at her reassuringly. She gave me a glance, then slowly handed me the child.

"Eve. Her name is Eve," the mother explained as the child was placed in my arms. I nodded and noticed she stopped crying with me holding her. It made me feel special.

"Eve," I whisper.

The mother gave her child one more smile before leaving with momma. One of the older girls guided us back underneath the bed, and I held Eve close to me, not wanting to let go. "What's going on?" Asked one of the older boys. Eve and I hid in the small corner and I found it weird that she had a boy blanket wrapped around her with boy toys like trucks. It wasn't girly, but different. I liked it.

There was screaming outside the door, but I felt safe and not afraid with Eve with me. The other kids stepped out and left the room. They left the door open, but I couldn't see anything from underneath the bed. It seemed like forever, but I felt an urge to search for them. They shouldn't have left. I placed Eve safely in the corner. "Quiet, Eve," I requested of her. "I'll be right back." I dusted myself off and peeked out of the corner of the door.

Faint screams sounded, and I slowly walked out. "Momma?" I called out and peeked around every corner. There was lots of screaming and shouts from below. I peeked through the balcony bars to see lines of people unclothed and they were all covered in blood. I heard loud pops that made me cover my ears. The fully-clothed men had guns pointed at the people covered in blood. I continued down the hall in search of momma.

"Mom?" I shouted louder and heard thumping upstairs. I quickly ran into the bathroom and peeked around the corner. The armed men invaded my bedroom, and my heart began to pound at the thought of Eve still there lying under the bed. I should have taken her with me. Some others turned down the hall my way, and I hid behind the bathroom door.

I waited a good 10 minutes until the footsteps proceeded downstairs. I hurried into the bedroom, and I crawled under my bed. "Eve?" I whispered searching every crook and cranny but seeing she's nowhere. "Eve!" My heart pounded against my chest and I turned around. She has to be somewhere!

I dashed off into the hall and opened the door to one of the rooms. One man was inside, watching a girl unclothe herself. She cried. I shut the door and continued down the hall until I reached the staircase leading to the basement. I didn't bother to cover my tracks, as I only cared about one thing. As I reached the bottom of the basement, I heard child-like giggling that made me feel better. Some ladies rushed by me, one tugging at the other and begging for nonsense.

I followed the sound of the child and peeked into the room. There stood a girl holding a pink blanket. For a split second, the girl holding the child glanced at me, but my eyes were glued on the child. It's not Eve. I turned around and headed back upstairs. She's got to be somewhere.

"Please, please!" I saw the ladies previously in the presence of a man. The one that tugged at the other is now in the hand of a large man, the other pleads. The man's blue eyes held nothing but hatred, and he dropped the girl to the ground. She didn't get up after that, and the other cried hysterically as the man gazed upon her.

Before they could notice my presence, I ran toward the back door and reached the outside world. There was a fire burning off in the distance, followed by agonizing cries. Everything began to dawn on me at that instant, and tears burned my eyes. I ran and ran. I didn't stop. I could see the field of people and momma was nowhere to be found. My breath became labored, and in the heap of clothes, I could see a white blanket on top. It was now dirty, and I still could recognize the trucks and boy designs on it.

Eve.

•Chapter 17•

Theadora Sanford•

I gripped the blade in my hand and took breaths. Tears stained my eyes as the blade neared my wrist. I bit my tongue as the cut pierced my flesh. I watched the blood pour out and began to count. I did it every time, and I didn't know why. It was almost like counting my final moments if those were to be my final seconds. I groaned and seethed air. It was early in the morning. I didn't know how Josh would feel about this, but I couldn't explain the relief I found.

"1.... 2..." I slid my back against the door and stared at my bleeding wrist.

"Thea, are you alright?" Josh knocked on the door and shook me out of my state. "I smell blood... are you on your period?" My face heated as he mentioned my period and I couldn't think of any excuse. I didn't want to lie to Josh.

"I'll be out in a moment," I excused. He stopped knocking and I heard him walk away. Why was he up so early? I quickly grabbed a tissue to wipe away the shameful blood I shed. I rinsed the blade under the sink and ended up tripping as I rushed back to the toilet. My back landed on the cold floor and I groaned in pain.

"Thea?" Josh questioned from outside the door.

I quickly shouted, "I'm fine!" I flushed the bloody tissue down the toilet and wrapped my wrist in even more tissue. I couldn't get it to stop bleeding. I opened the door and turned off the light. "I just fell," I whispered and rushed over to the bed. Josh was crouched over the bed putting on one of his shoes. "Why are you up early?" I whispered covering my body with the blanket.

"Well," he rubbed the back of his neck. "I was going to surprise you for when you woke up, but you're already awake."

I nodded but then tilted to my head, "Surprise me? Why?"

He gave me a funny look, "It's your birthday."

Realization struck me, and I slid even farther into the bed. "Oh."

He cocked an eyebrow, "You don't seem so happy for your 17th birthday, huh, babe?" I flushed as he called me a nickname for the first time. The type of names I heard couples in the pack call one another.

"I am, it's just early. I'm quite tired," I tried to avoid the subject.

He kissed my forehead, "well, are you on your period? I can go out and grab some toiletries for you."

I felt uncomfortable as he mentioned it and pulled the covers over my head in embarrassment. "N-No, I'm not on my..." I stopped and heard him laugh in amusement. He tugged the blanket off of me and sniffed.

"Did you hurt yourself, then?" He trailed his nose to my hand and grabbed it. My eyes widened as he turned it over and saw the fresh cut on my wrist. "Thea..." He whispered in a low tone. I couldn't see his eyes, or hear the emotion in his voice. I couldn't tell if he were angry, sad, confused, or worried, or worse. I assumed he was outraged. Things like this make him mad.

"J-Josh..." I whispered.

When he looked up, I wished I could take it all back. He wasn't sad, worried, confused, or even pissed off. He was simply... disappointed. "Did you do this to yourself?" He demanded. I gulped and willed myself not to cry. I shouldn't be crying if I did this to myself. He took my silence for an answer. "Thea... why?"

I looked away, "I...I'm sorry," I whispered slowly pulling my hand away from him and cradling it against my body.

"No, Thea, tell me. I want to help you." He leaned over my fragile figure. I couldn't stand the way he spoke. It made me ashamed of myself. "I see scars from the other times," he added.

"Josh, I..." I paused and continued to not reach his gaze. "This is my life," I finally stated.

He sighed and his voice became stern, "Don't ever do this to yourself again. Do you hear me, Thea? I don't want you to be the cause of adding more scars to your precious body. I'm serious."

I slowly nodded, "yes."

"It may seem like it'll never end, baby, but I promise it will. I'm here to help." Josh surprisingly wrapped his arm around me comfortingly and pulled me closer and kissed the top of my head. "Don't apologize," he added sharply.

I leaned into him, finding it hard to believe he existed. I couldn't ask for anyone better to call my mate, to call mine.

'''

"Happy birthday!" Riley ran up to me with a plate in hand. Upon it was a single slice of cake with a lit match stuck into it as a candle replacement.

"You know my birthday?" I gasped as I accepted her sweet gift.

She grinned, "Remember when I said I've known you longer than you think?" She whipped out a fork out of her pocket, and I gladly accepted the slice of cake. I hadn't seen Josh after he left early in the morning. I was afraid he wasn't going to come back, but I couldn't hide the excitement I still had for my birthday.

"Thank you, Riley." I groaned in satisfaction as I downed the first bite. It was absolutely delicious. I loved her skills in the kitchen. "This is delightful!"

Riley seemed shocked that I enjoyed her meal, but how could I not? It was lovely. She hugged me tightly and cleared her throat, "Alpha requested to see you at the end of your day in the pack library."

I raised my eyebrows at what she said but nodded my head either way. We couldn't be seen speaking to one another for so long and have the others raise suspicions about us. We scuttled our separate ways and I stopped in the middle of the hall.

"Thea, hey, you!" Jake waved to me. I hurried over and bowed.

"Alpha Jake."

"Don't address him as that. He is the Alpha of nothing!" Beta Bryce stumbled down the hall a drunken mess. "I am your master, you hear me?"

"Yes, B-Beta Bryce," I whispered in fear as he approached Jake and I. I kept my head down.

"Now, Omega, tell me; why are you wearing a scarf around your neck inside the house? Do you not get enough warmth from the AC?"

I stiffened and averted my gaze. "I-I was cold, sorry. I do not have air conditioning in my room."

"There's AC here, so take it off. I need something to wrap this." He held up his hand. On it was a wide cut that spewed blood.

"Disgusting," Jake gagged.

"I-I can patch it up for you," I offered.

"Stop fucking stuttering, omega." I swallowed. "Give me your damn scarf. If I wanted you to bandage it I'd tell you to, do not be disobedient, omega."

If I do it, he'll be sure to notice. I have to protect Josh. I took a deep breath and looked up for once in my life.

"No."

Beta Bryce and Jake looked completely taken by surprise. "E-Excuse me?"

"Did I stutter?"

Before I could comprehend, Beta Bryce's fist landed on my eye. I turned away and covered my face. "You dare to disobey me, slave?" He growled grabbing my by my arm and yanking me up.

He threw me against the wall, and the snap of my arm brought tears to my eyes. "Who do you think you are?" He talked and yanked the scarf. It tightened around my neck to the point where I couldn't breathe. I clawed at it until it untied, and I fell against the floor.

Scarf in hand, Bryce narrowed his eyes at me. I scooted back against the wall as he gazed my neck. "Is that a mark, omega?"

"It's," I gasped using my arm that wasn't broken to support myself. "none of your business."

"Enough! Enough! Enough!" Jake shouted, but Beta Bryce had enough. He shifted and his eyes bled red. "I said stop!" Jake grabbed Bryce's fur, but he reistsed until he broke free.

"By the heavens in me stop this instant, Bryce!" The alpha voice made everyone freeze, and when I turned over, I saw Alpha Alexander.

I looked down at the ground and heard Bryce shift back to his regular form. "Omega, come with me," Alpha requested. I didn't dare to disobey any longer, so I stood up and limped over to his side. "Clean up, both of you, and don't speak of this."

He pointed to both Jake and Bryce, then escorted me down the hall. His hand was placed against the small of my back, and I knew that Beta Bryce would never let this go, and I would be punished for it later.

"I'm not sorry," I mumbled lowly as he opened the door to the library.

"Do not speak," he demanded gently in his alpha voice, and I obeyed. He sat me at the desk and pulled out a first aid kit. He proceeded to open it and take out a cloth.

He sprayed one substance on it, then gently placed it against my eye. I flinched a little but allowed him to. "Hold this," he remained concentrated and I took over by holding it against my own eye.

His dark eyes seemed to lighten a little, and it was almost as if staring at someone familiar. Alpha Alexander spotted my mark and his eyes turned black like usual. "Bryce?" He asked as he gripped my arm.

"No," I confessed. I hoped he wouldn't ask who's mark it was. Before I could say anything, he yanked my broken arm out and pushed up with so much force I heard a pop. I yelped in pain and a few tears fell from my eyes.

"You'll be fine," he stood up after wrapping my arm in a bandage. I placed the cloth down.

"Thank you," I whispered.

"Toady, it's your birthday?" he asked without looking at me. He turned to a row of the books on the shelf and I furrowed my eyebrows.

"Y-Yes. I'm 17."

He let out a breath, "You're a woman."

I cleared my throat. I hoped he didn't have any intentions with me. Luna Erica would be pissed. "Yes, sir," I grumbled.

He turned around and unlocked one of the drawers in the desk. I watched him carefully as he pulled out a small rectangular-shaped gift. It had pink wrapping paper, topped with a black bow. "Where would you like me to deliver this?" I asked as he handed it to me.

"No one. It's yours."

My throat became dry, and I froze on the spot. "M-me?" I pointed to myself, unable to understand why he'd get me anything. How did he even know it was my birthday?

"Go ahead. Open it." Alpha Alexander ushered me. I felt my heart sink. I could only think of all the terrible things he could give me. I've never had a good surprise in my life, and I could only imagine anything worse in this gift. I slowly tore the paper apart as I held my breath.

My breath hitched as I realized it wasn't anything I'd been expecting. It was hard, and it sparked my interest. A book. "Great Expectations," I read the title as I lifted it up to my eye level.

"I saw you looking at it in the library awhile ago. I figured you wanted to read it."

"Sir, I-I, thank you." I was unsure of what to do. I put my good arm around him in an awkward side hug. "I'll return it as soon as I finish reading it."

Alpha Alexander shook his head, "Don't. It's yours. Keep it."

My eyebrows drew together, "A-Are you sure?"

"Yes, and I'll read it to you if you have any issues." His proposition seemed too good to be true. All he ever did was abuse me and treat me poorly. Why was he so nice suddenly?

A sad smile reached my lips. I wished mama could be here to read it. I loved the voices she did. "My mom used to read to me," I whispered.

"Did she?"

I nodded, "Yes. She passed when I was young, and I miss her more than anything."

Tears blurred my vision, but I blinked them back. "She... She was an amazing woman," Alpha Alexander stated.

I looked up at him in shock, "You... You knew my mother?"

I stared into his dark eyes, but they seemed to become lighter. "Theadora, I more than knew Vera." Confusion washed over me. At the mention of her name, I stared into a mirror. His eyes were a dark, crystal-like blue that is just like my own.

•*Chapter 18*•

Theadora Sanford•

It seemed to happened in slow motion. The book fell from my hands, and I couldn't find any words to describe how I felt. "Y-You're m-my..." His silence answered my question. I took steps back, unable to process anything. "No," I whispered continuing to back up.

"Theadora, watch out," Alpha Alexander attempted to catch me, but I hit the bookcase from backing up so much. A few of the books fell, and he growled in frustration.

My heart sped in my chest and Alpha Alexander held out his hand for me, "Please allow me to explain."

I pushed his hand away in anger and stood back up, "Explain what! Why you abused me for all my life? Why you left my mother on her own? Why you let these things continue to happen to me?" Furious tears shed from my eyes. "You," I pointed to him shaking my head, "are not my father."

"Thea, I know it's a lot to take in." I ground my teeth and looked up at the ceiling. I silently prayed. I prayed all of this could be fixed. I needed mama. What would she do? I took in a deep breath and straightened myself. "Will you calm down for me to explain?" I avoided his gaze and walked over to the desk. I sat down in the chair and expectantly gazed at him. Alpha Alexander sighed, yet remained at a distance. "18 years ago I went to a pack. I was just on a visit to settle disputes between the Alpha of the pack and I. The Alpha allowed me to dinner with his pack members, and that's when I smelled it."

"Smelled?"

He nodded, "yes, I smelled her before I saw her. It was this strong scent of-of beauty. I-I cannot explain it, but it was so enticing. I remember staring at the door, and then she walked out. Long brown hair and green eyes. She walked so gracefully, but I don't think she noticed me. I was 17 at the time, and she was 15. She set my plate in front of me, and I grabbed her wrist. She was surprised, I suppose. She felt the... the sensation of tingles. It was almost like... like magic.

Our moment didn't last long because the Alpha dismissed her, but she stared at me the entire time she walked back. She tripped over a few things. It was cute."

I couldn't help but laugh with the tears in my eyes. "She was clumsy," I looked down and played with the fabric of my dress.

"I tell you, I didn't believe in the Moon Goddess until she blessed me with a mate. I don't know why she'd do it, though. Me, of all people, getting a mate." I nodded in agreement. Mama deserved better. "Anyway, after dinner I waited outside the doors waiting for her. I could just smell her scent growing stronger and stronger. I was so excited to see her again. Everyone had left, so when she came out, I grabbed her by the waist. She kind of screamed in surprise, but relaxed because she knew it was me. I kissed her then, and she seemed just as happy as me. I brought her to my room, and that night we..."

"I-I know." I quickly intervened. I didn't want to hear about either mama or Alpha Alexander having sex.

"The next morning we got caught. It was by the Alpha's beta. Vera was still asleep, but I waved him off until he told me who she was. An omega. I was already settling some issues with the Alpha, and if he found out I was sleeping with his Omega, it would ruin my own reputation as an Alpha. They'd think I was weak. I made him swear not to tell, and I luckily didn't mention we were mates. I started getting dressed when she woke up. She smiled at me then asked where I was going. That's when I... I told her to leave. At first, she was confused, then... then I grabbed her by her neck and I carried her outside my room. I dropped her-I fucking dropped her like nothing! Like she meant nothing to me!"

I was shaking in anger. I wanted to hit him. I wanted to make him feel the pain of rejection he gave my mom. I wanted him to pay. "You're sick," I shook my head and stood up.

"Thea, I know you're angry, but please let me finish."

"Why should I? You've been making me do everything you've wanted all your life!" I stood in outrage.

"You're right, and this is one time of all I'm not making you do anything. All I beg is that you listen." I sighed and sat back down with my arms crossed.

"I finished my business with the pack and went home. I didn't know she was pregnant. Months after I went home I couldn't get my mind off of her. I wanted to see her. So I did. I didn't make my presence known, so I killed a few guards. I climbed through a window. It was easy to slip into because there were bushes covering it and I don't even think the Alpha knew of the secret entrance. I saw her. She was in her 3rd trimester and I assumed it wasn't mine and I got angry. I-I slapped her and threatened to kill the baby -- you. She told me I wasn't the father, and she hated me that time. I apologized to her profusely. I ended up leaving, but my anger resided in my head. I gathered a group of my best soldiers. I told them we were going to take over the pack. I told them to kill everyone that resided there but to leave the maids alone. We invaded them by surprise, and my soldiers made them strip before killing them so they could donate the clothes to charity or some bullshit like that."

"Was mama there?"

He nodded, "Yes, and she was with her sister. Her sister was trying to pull her back. She didn't know we were mates, but that's when it happened -- she allowed the words of rejection to leave her lips and I heard my own heart breaking."

"Good! You bastard!" I finally shouted.

He flinched at my words, yet he continued, "It angered me. I had been rejected by my mate. A once in a lifetime chance at true love. I killed her sister in front of her. She screamed that she hated me the entire time, but I was blinded by my anger. Eyes black and all. I demanded to see you, but she was in tears by then. She begged me not to hurt you, but I didn't care. I crashed into her room and saw a girl holding you. Your cousin, Riley."

I felt a lump form in my throat as her previous words rang in my ears. "I've known you longer than you think."

"I pushed her aside and held you for the first time. You were so gentle. You had a pink blanket wrapped around you and you were giggling. When you saw me you smiled, and my wolf was telling me that your mother was a liar, and you were mine. I could tell by your eyes, along with your scent. I couldn't hurt you. I locked the three of you in the room and my men finished off everyone else. Few escaped, but I moved in my own pack members and stayed to protect your mother and you."

"Protect us? You never protected us! My mom was sick and she died! You abuse me! Everyone in this pack abuses me! I was raped, for Christ's sake!"

"Thea, I had no idea-" he paused, "Y-you were what?" His eyes turned black like they normally were.

"Beta Bryce raped me on several occasions. Is that what you wanted? You were so hurt my mother rejected you that you want your own daughter to suffer? In that case, I'm glad she rejected you! You don't deserve any chance at love."

"I didn't know he took advantage of you!"

"But you know he hits me! You let it happen, whether you intended it or not."

"I'll make sure he doesn't-"

"And Jake. Jake is my brother?"

He shook his head, "No, he's pretending to be my son for the sake of Bryce not being Alpha."

I laughed, "So you'd have a replacement be Alpha instead of telling the world who your actual heir is? I'm glad. I could never take place of this damned pack."

He sighed, "I miss her just as much of you. The guilt has been weighing on me ever since I found out she passed. I never expected it. If I had a second chance, I would never have left the two of you."

"I can't." I stood up and stared at the book on the ground. I gave it a sour look and picked up. I threw it at him angrily and shouted, "I hate you!" I stormed out of the library with furious tears flying out of my eyes.

I stormed downstairs and reached my bedroom. "Hey-- what's wrong?" Josh looked up.

"Take me. Take me anywhere. I just don't want to be here. Take me away. Let's go. We can travel the world. We can go to Paris, Manhattan, Venice, anywhere!" I cried.

Josh furrowed his eyebrows. "Are you sure?"

"Yes, Josh, please," I begged.

He helped me climb out the window and I felt my heart pounding in my chest. He took my hand and we began to run. I didn't turn back, nor did I stop.

• • •

"We're here," Josh panted and bent over his knees in heavy breaths. I looked up at the home, and I nodded. It'll have to do for now.

"I can't go back there," I admitted.

Josh frowned, "I'll get the rest of our stuff early in the morning. You won't have to."

I grinned and hugged him, "thank you, Josh." My heart started to feel heavy. I wished he never told me the truth. How will Riley feel knowing I've left her behind? So many thoughts raced through my head, and the guilt of running away slowly grew.

"What made you change your mind?" interrogated Josh.

"Can we go inside, please? I need to lie down." I avoided the subject. I would talk about it later, but for now, I needed a refreshing drink and silence to clear my head.

"Of course." Josh opened the back window and boosted me up into the circulated home. He was next and made sure to shut the window behind him. The sudden warmth made goosebumps form along my arm and I massaged them. "Come," Josh gently guided me by hand to the living room. I sat down on the sofa and he placed a pillow beneath my head. "Do you need anything?"

I nodded, "Yes, please, a drink."

He nodded and scurried away. I couldn't help but laugh a little at the sudden change in our roles. Now, Josh is taking care of me, unlike me taking care of him and everyone else. I heard the sound of a glass being filled, then a fridge opening and shutting. Josh rushed back over with a glass in hand that had some type of pink liquid. "Don't worry," he tilted it slowly to me with it pressed against my lips. I slowly drank the liquid, but as I tasted the fruitiness I ended up taking the glass and finishing it myself. "It's fruit punch," Josh stated.

"It's delicious, thank you." I grinned at Josh and he kissed my forehead.

"Are you ready to talk about it?" His eyes brightened expectantly. I bit my lip hesitantly, then I looked down at my lap. "Thea," Josh lifted my head by my chin, "tell me what's going. Please let me help you."

His eyes held concern, so I finally sighed, "A-Alpha Alexander is my... dad."

"What?"

I growled, "he's my dad."

"So you're... a descendant?"

I frowned, "I suppose so. He said Jake is pretending to be his son."

His eyes lightened, "Thea, do you know what this means!"

I furrowed my eyebrows, "N-No."

"You can lead this pack. You can make a home here. We can make a home."

Josh grabbed my arm, but I pulled away from him. "Are you insane? I just told you Alpha Alexander is my father and you want to jump aboard and make me into a leader? I can't do that, and especially not to them! They permanently scarred me mentally, emotionally, and physically! I want nothing to do with them!"

He paused, "Thea, it's not like that. You make the rules this time, and you're the boss. You can put that asshole Bryce in pack prison for life and anyone that has mistreated you. You can be the boss, now."

Me? A servant? A slave? An Omega? "This is too much." I turned away. My head was now swarming with thoughts again, and it made me feel sick. I hurried to the bathroom and bent over the toilet and let it all out. Tears dampened my eyes as Josh pulled back my hair away from me. I flushed the toilet and rinsed my mouth.

"I'm sorry, Thea," Josh sighed. "I just haven't had a pack in so long, the thought of it just excited me. I was way in over my head." I gargled the mouthwash beside the sink to get rid of the awful taste in my mouth.

"You think?"

He still seemed upset, "I'll get the rest of our belongings in the morning and we can go anywhere."

I hugged him tightly, "thank you, Josh. I love you."

He wrapped his arm around me, "I love you too. Now, when was the last time you shifted?"

His question caught me by surprise, "Years ago! Not since I first shifted!"

"Well," he leaned into my ear, "let's change that."

"Wha-" he grabbed my hand and pulled me out of the bathroom.

"Josh, I couldn't-" he continued until we reached the front door. "I need shoes!" I exclaimed as he swung open the door.

"You don't need shoes in wolf form. C'mon!" He ushered me over to the grass and sat down and stared at me. "Go on," he waved his hand.

"Josh, I can't," I bit my lip nervously. "It's been so long."

"Channel your wolf. Focus on the two of you, and I'll always be here if you need me."

His words left me hanging because I didn't even know my wolf. I couldn't even remember her name. I breathed in and out and shut my eyes. 'You there?'

'Yes,' replied Josh, and I opened my eyes.

"Not you," I frowned.

"You're channeling the wrong person, here." he informed.

I closed my eyes again and concentrated on my wolf alone. The small details of her I could remember. Her shiny black fur, and curled claws. Her razor-sharp teeth and pointed snout. 'Patience is a virtue, and a virtue is righteous.' came a feminine voice inside my head.

'Hello?' I greeted.

'It's nice to speak to you after so long, Theadora. My name is Naomi.'

'Naomi? You have a beautiful name.'

'Thank you, dear. What do you summon me for?' She sounded graceful and sophisticated.

'I want to shift.' I requested.

'It'll be painful, but if that's what you want.' My eyes opened suddenly, and I fell on my knees.

I felt my bones shifting slowly into their positions, and I willed myself not to cry. Each bone bent in opposite directions and I fell onto all fours as my spine twisted out of shape. I cried out in pain as my bones continued to shift into position. Small pores around my body expanded and out grew small sprouts of black fur. My hand bent to a claw, and soon after, more bones popped into position. I closed my eyes and endured the pain until it all just

stopped.

I felt the cool air tickled my face, and my bones no longer ached from the shift. Did it work? I still felt normal. I peeked open my eye and met Josh's. His jaw was on the floor as he stared at me. "What's wrong?" I tried to ask, but it came out in a rough bark. I looked down and stared at 2 furry paws. My heart soared at the sight.

"Thea," Josh gasped as he walked over to me. Excitedly, I barked and ran in a small circle. "you're gorgeous." He pet my fur and I felt his warmth. It made me happy.

'I want to run,' I announced ecstatically.

'Wait for me.' Josh crouched down to shift, but I still ran off into the woods. My paws collided with the fresh grass that was lifted from the snow. I licked out my tongue and wove my way through the trees as if I'd known them my entire life. I could hear Josh gaining up on me, so I pushed myself to run faster. I grinned and took a sharp turn, only to be met by his presence and I ran into him. We rolled over until I was on top of him, so I licked his face. He gave me a playful scowl and I nuzzled my face to his fur.

I have never been so happy. I have never felt so free.

•*Chapter 19*•

Bryce Jole•

"It's settled," I sat back and kicked my feet up on my desk. It's just a matter of time until Jake drops dead by "chance" and I get to fulfill my role as Alpha. It's all I truly want, and I deserve it.

My wolf has been itching for me to punish the girl for daring to speak back to me. It's a shame Alexander had to stop by and stop anything further from happening. If he wasn't Alpha I'd have her punished so horribly she'd beg to die. I'd deal with it later.

"Beta Bryce, you requested to see me?" The girl opened the door to my office with her head lowered.

"I need some relief," I unbuckled my belt and sat back for her.

"B-But sir, I-I'm not-"

"Do I need to say it again? I'm getting frustrated with the disobedience today." I growled. The girl began to shake, and my wolf watched in confusion.

'This girl,' he noted. She slowly trudged over and bent down on her knees. She turned her head away with tears in her eyes.

"Sir, please," her voice quivered and she looked up at me with glossy green eyes. My heart stopped in that moment, and I paused.

'Mate.'

She seemed unaffected by gazing into my eyes. No. Mates aren't real. They don't exist. "What's your name?" I questioned lifting her chin up to my eyes. She looked down. "Don't look down," I requested softly.

"My name is Riley. Riley Sanford, sir."

'Her wolf doesn't notice.' My wolf pointed out. I pulled my pants back up and buckled up.

"Leave," I demanded and turned away from her.

"Sir," she touched my arm, and I stared at it in horror. She made my heart flutter and her voice made me feel warm inside. I couldn't keep my eyes off of her hand as it touched my skin. "I-I'm sorry," she retracted her hand and it left a searing and empty feeling inside. She hurried out of the room before I could process anything further.

'What do I do with her?' I asked my wolf.

'I have no idea,' he shivered in pleasure, 'but don't let her go.'

I frowned because I didn't have time for a mate. I figured I'd need a Luna, but I never expected to get a mate of my own. 'Bryce, we must speak immediately.' Alexander snapped me out of my thoughts, and I was glad he did. I didn't want to overthink about the girl.

'I have time,' I replied sitting back up on my desk and placing my elbows atop.

'You have time? I think you mean you'll make time, Beta.' Alexander growled harshly. I rolled my eyes. All the leverage the old piece of dust had was his Alpha tone. Besides that, he was nothing. Weak. Just as weak as the Omega.

"Yes, Alpha,' I replied sarcastically, but he was too stupid to notice.

'In my offic-' He opened the door and frowned at me. "Why aren't I surprised?"

I chuckled, "We've been over this, Alpha," I clasped my hands, "I'll be in your place soon. I'm just adjusting."

"Up," he ordered. "Have you forgotten Jake-"

"I did the research, Alexander, and you are not the father." I dropped the file on my desk. I knew there was no way in hell he could have had a son. He didn't even like Erica. He just used her to look better as an Alpha.

He grinned at me in satisfaction. I raised my eyebrows, confused on why he would be so damn content. I just exposed his lies, and all he can do is laugh it off. He exploded into full blown laughter crouched over and all. He slapped his knee and even wiped a few tears. "What's so funny?" I ground my teeth.

Alexander rolled his eyes, "Big deal, you caught my lie. That still doesn't mean you'll be Alpha."

I chuckled, "Well, I was going to have someone kill off Jake for me, but then I kind of thought: Why would you have a kid in the first place? Erica's never been pregnant, and the two of you don't even have a functional relationship."

"You had someone take a blood test? How did you even draw my blood?"

"You're a deep sleeper, grandpa," I placed my hands behind my head.

"Well, at this point I'm done lying. I'm done lying to everyone."

I sighed, "Well, that makes my transition so much easier."

"I'm not finished, Bryce. I'm here to tell you the truth. I do have an heir. In fact, she's been living under your nose all her life."

"Her?" I frowned. This old bat has got to be lying.

"Theadora Sanford," he stated. My wolf buckled up.

"Who?" I asked.

His eyes darkened, "Who? Theadora Sanford is the girl you've abused your entire your life. Theadora Sanford is my daughter. Theadora Sanford is the Omega. Theadora Sanford is the girl you raped. Theadora Sanford is your Luna."

This time, I laughed. I mean, the hell is he going on about? The Omega being a luna? That's priceless. I bent over because my chest started to hurt from all the laughing. "What's so funny? I have all the documentation. Look in the drawer on the bottom right." Alexander tossed a key on the desk, and I grabbed it. Does he expect me to believe this? "Take a blood test if you need anything more to convince yourself."

I opened the drawer and saw a few files. I grabbed the first one, and in it was a picture of a pretty hot girl. Verana Sanford. There was a bright red stamp marked DECEASED across the top. "That's... that's her mother." Alexander sounded breathless as he said it, but I tossed it aside and picked up the other file. I shifted through the documents, reading all the official markings on the girl. The Omega. Alexander's daughter.

"Well," I dropped the file on op of his desk. "Isn't that... unexpected?"

"She's next in line. Not you, Bryce."

I raised my eyebrow, "That girl can't even look a roach in the eyes, and you want her to be an Alpha? She can't even fucking speak in complete sentences. Does she even know you're her dad?" I almost shouted.

"Yes, I just told her."

"And..?"

"She.... ran away. Why should that even be important? She's my daughter and you ripped her from her innocence."

"I'm no saint, Alexander, but I know damn well as a father you're the biggest failure in her life, because, with you, she was in this position. If you didn't treat her like shit in the first place she would be raised properly."

He scoffed, "and suddenly you're not in the wrong?"

"No, but I know a thing or two about deadbeat dads. I hate that girl with my entire existence. I couldn't care less if she died right now. Matter of fact, I'll have her killed as soon as possible. She's nothing. She's weak. She has no power. She's scared of me." I crossed my arms and grinned in satisfaction.

Alexander didn't reply and I searched through the drawer again. I opened the next file, and my heart dropped. "Who-Who's this?" I whispered. Where did he get this?

Alexander looked over, "That's Riley, her cousin."

•Theadora Sanford•

"Josh," I groaned. I poked him over and over again. I wasn't enjoying the movie.

"Yes, baby?"

I felt my face heat up. "I don't like this movie. People are dying," I frowned.

"It's my favorite movie. Just watch it and you won't be disappointed by the end." He refused to make eye contact and I groaned in frustration. I continued to poke him. "Thea, stop." Stubbornly, I started to poke his chest and I crawled over him. "Thea-" he paused as I kissed his lips gently. He pulled away, "that's it." He turned over so that he was above me and he pinned my hands above me. "You're being a bad girl, Thea."

I frowned and bit my lip because he looked adorable when he was frustrated. "No, don't do that." He leaned down and started to kiss my neck. I arched my back and moaned softly at the simple contact. "Josh," I gasped as he nibbled on my neck. He stopped kissing my neck and pulled back, a serious expression on his face.

"Thea, I don't think you should run away."

I gave him a funny look, "What? That's all you've ever wanted."

He nodded, "Yes, but this is your time to show them what you're made of. It's not about leading your abusers, it's showing them the light."

"There is no light." I pulled away from his grip and looked away from him. I didn't see how he could just fall back on everything he told me. Running away was all he wanted!

"Thea," he called gently. I continued to look down. "Thea, look at me." I crossed my arms to show him I wasn't going to falter. "Please, baby?" I sighed and finally gazed into his gorgeous gray eyes. "You have a chance to change the world by doing this, and you may not believe me," he caressed my cheek carefully. "You definitely changed me, Thea. I would have never thought I'd fall in love with someone other than my mate." My heart constricted at his words. "I know it'll be tough, but this could possibly save future Omegas and servants or whoever from the same thing you went through."

"No," I brought my brows together. "If I were to lead the pack, there would be no Omega. Everyone would be equal, not including the higher ranks. There shouldn't be any role less than a member of the pack."

A cute grin formed on Josh's face, "that's a place to start."

"Josh, do you think we can do this?" I whispered in fear.

"I know we can, baby."

I bit my lip, "Beta Bryce... he wants to be Alpha. He won't like it."

Josh was outraged, "His opinion doesn't matter. He has no dominion over you." He gazed at me with concern and kissed my lips softly. "You're no longer their slave -- their... toy."

I slowly nodded and grinned at Josh. I felt safe with him around. "I appreciate you, Josh, and everything you have done and will do for me."

He paused and stared at me. He kissed my neck, "Thank you for that, baby. I love you."

"I need to go back there. I need to stand up to them."

He laughed, "easy there, Luna, I don't want you to blindly walk into something like that."

I rolled my eyes, "I'll be fine, Joshua. I just need to do it alone. I'll be okay." I stated confidently.

"Joshua? Where'd you get that from?" He cocked an eyebrow.

I blushed, "It-It was on the nametag. The one on the kitchen counter." I looked down.

"Oh? So you've been reading excellently? Eyes up here, lovely." I faced him and he grinned, "So... you want to run there in wolf form? I bet this time I can beat you."

I shoved him aside and hopped out of bed. "Gotta be quicker than that!" I laughed.

• • •

I put on the pair of clothes Josh brought for me from the cabin. I actually managed to beat him by a lot this time. I'm small and fast.

I never knew I was so light on my feet in wolf form. I dusted myself off just as Riley burst into the room. "Thea!" She wrapped her arms around me.

"Huh?" I asked.

"Oh God, is it true? Alpha Alexander... he's... he's your.."

Slowly, I nodded. "How did you find out?"

She exclaimed, "He just announced it to the entire pack, and you're next in line to be Luna." My chest started to ache, and I looked away from her. "I-I can't believe-"

"Yeah, no one can, cupcake." A voice from the doorway butted in. I looked up and spotted Bryce in the arch of the door with a knife in hand. He was playing with it as he stared at Riley. She took a step in front of me.

"Don't touch her," Riley demanded.

"I'm not here for you. I want to talk to the girl. The so-called "daughter" of Alexander." Riley gazed between us, and I took her hand.

"I don't want you to get hurt. You should go," I whispered.

"What about-"

"I'll be fine. He's on his way," I assured. Riley finally nodded and left the room. Bryce turned back to stare at her and I cleared my throat.

"Who's the he?"

"None of your business," I snapped back. My heart was speeding up at each remark. I couldn't believe I was speaking back to him. "You can't stop me from being Luna, and the first thing I'll do is lock you away in the pack prison forever. You can't hurt me. Not anymore."

He chuckled, "Just because you act strong doesn't mean you are." He took steps toward me, and I took equal steps back. "You're still scared of me. I have power over you." My back hit the wall and he stopped just a single step away from me. "I promise you'll never get a chance to be Luna. Not as long as I'm around." He pointed the knife at my neck and grinned at the mark. "You can't stop me. No one can." Bryce turned away and whistled a tune as he left. My heart was beating out of my chest and I glared at his back. He was right. I had no control over him. I was weak.

Josh dropped down with only a pair of shorts and he saw me. "What's wrong?" he asked.

"Bryce," I whispered, "he's going to kill me."

•Chapter 20•

Theadora Sanford•

I woke up cold and alone. I turned over to find comfort from Josh, but I fell off the bed instead. The fall shocked me, and I immediately sat up. "Josh?" I asked. I searched around my room to find that he was nowhere in sight. "Josh!" I yelled knocking on the bathroom door, and it creaked open upon my touch. The bathroom was empty, so I turned off into the main hall. "Riley, have you seen Josh?" I knocked on her shoulder.

She squeaked at my presence and turned around with a hand on her heart. "Yes, I did. He left early in the morning. He was upset about something," she informed.

I sighed in relief. I was afraid Bryce or someone else had got to him. "Thank you," I turned back and hurried back into my room. I dragged a chair over to the window and stood on top of it to climb out. The chilling air blew at my hair and I bent down and shifted. It was quicker and smoother. There was less pain. I stretched myself before I leaped off and ran.

I didn't know exactly where the cabin was, but Josh's scent was strong since he didn't use a masker. He either forgot or didn't care. I pounded through the forest with one person on my mind, and my heart set out to find him. I hoped he wasn't in pain or worse. My heart was pounding so heard I thought it would break free out of my chest and take a life of its own.

'Josh?' I called as I stopped in front of the house. I shifted back and noticed the door wide open. I helped myself and walked inside the house. I spotted a torn shirt. I quickly threw it on and followed my ears to the sound of crashing and glass shattering against the wooden floors. "Josh!" I yelled cupping my hands over my mouth.

I reached the opening into one of the other living areas and spotted Josh. His hands were claws and his eyes were yellow. I'd never seen anything like it. His teeth were canines, and he had no shirt on. I hurried over to him, but he stepped away from me growling. "What's wrong?" I asked as I neared him.

He growled in response, "Don't get near me."

"Tell me," I ordered as I stepped toward him.

"Thea, I don't want to hurt you. Stop now," his voice was growls, but I could tell what he was saying.

I stopped in my tracks and surveyed our surroundings. There was broken glass and torn paper all across the floor. A lot of the furniture was spread across the room ripped or broken apart. "What happened?"

Josh remained silent as his chest heaved up and down. He glared at me in anger. "He. Can't. hurt. You."

"Josh," I whispered softly as I continued to step to him. "He won't," I tried to reassure him. "Not now, not ever."

"You're mine." He growled reaching out and grabbing my arm roughly. he pulled me toward him with my back pressed against his chest. He had his arms around my waist and he held me tightly.

"I know, Josh," I whispered. "I'm all yours," I rubbed his arm and his claws poked at my flesh. I shivered as they retracted back into nails, and his breaths evened.

I relaxed as I realized it was him again. "I'll kill him," Josh grumbled. I turned around when he loosened his grip and I faced him. His eyes remained darkened with anger and I brushed his cheek.

"It's not necessary."

He growled, "Thea, you'll never be happy as long as he's alive. I'll kill him. You can't stop me." He ripped away from me and I figured his anger was getting the best of him again.

"Josh, it's okay. I'm fine."

"Thea, don't you understand? He will stop at nothing -- I mean nothing to be Alpha." He took my hand in his. "I'll kill him. he's done enough damage to you and to everyone."

I bit my lip and looked down. Josh said nothing during the silence, but I knew what he said was true. I nodded my head as tears glistened in my eyes, "Okay."

"Okay?" He repeated.

"It needs to be done," I looked up at him as a tear fell from my eye. I didn't know what to expect. Josh was strong, but Bryce was too. I didn't know what I'd do without Josh in my life. He was here to protect me, love me -- make me feel safe.

"Don't cry, Thea. I love you," he confessed kissing my forehead. "I love you, I love you, I love you." He hugged me tightly.

I sighed, "I can't help it. I-I don't want to lose you." I grumbled onto his chest, and he laughed. I hit his arm and pouted. It wasn't funny.

"Okay, okay, I'm sorry. You'll never lose me. I'm always right here." He pressed his hand against my heart. He paused, then winked as he poked my neck, "and here."

"Shut up!' I laughed hitting his arm again.

He kissed me once more, "Let's go back to that damn pack house and show them what we're made of."

I grinned, "sounds like a plan."

• • •

I looked down at my bare feet, then the pack house. This is where it all began. This is where I was born, abused, manipulated... taken advantage of. The anger and pain built up inside of me. I balled my fist just as Josh enveloped it with his hand. I wanted them to all pay. Everyone, including Alexander, for everything they did to me. The times they broke me down and made me feel worthless. The times I was deprived of my right to consent. The time I spent alone grieving for my mother. The hole in my heart that craved anything to fill it up. The part of me they took away. The part of me that no longer is me, but this self-loathing, desperate, weak human being they molded me to be.

Not anymore. That part of me is no longer. I'm never letting them do it to me again. Ever. I stormed onto the grass, ignoring the guards demanding that I turn back. I ground my teeth. "Bryce!" I yelled to the house. He wanted this. He wanted me to try and stand up to him. Alone, I know I couldn't take him on, but I had faith in Josh and God.

"Bryce Jole!" I shouted my abuser's name once more. Memories and moments flooded my mind. All the times Bryce mistreated and abused me. The times I made my blood worth being drawn because I blamed myself. The fear of looking anyone in the eyes because I was an Omega. No longer. I'm an Alpha's descendant. I have the Alpha blood coursing through my veins, and it has been all along.

The door to the house opened and Alexander stepped out. I glared at him and his gaze locked to Josh. "Thea?" He questioned.

"We're not here for you," I growled.

"Rogue." Alexander's eyes darkened to a midnight black, but I blocked him from Josh.

"Alexander, we're not here for you," I stated.

"We're here for the piece of shit Beta you call Bryce," Josh spoke out.

Alexander's eyes widened, "Thea, don't you realize Bryce will kill you? You must give this time!"

"I'm not the one that's battling him."

He gave Josh a questioning glance, "This? This is your backup? You have a team of guards and soldiers willing to die for you over anything right now, and you pick a single rogue?" He shouted.

"This isn't their battle. It's mine."

"He'll kill this rogue within seconds, then come after you!"

"Why have guards woken me from my beauty sleep?" Bryce stepped out of the house, and I completely ignored Alexander and his pleas. There was nothing that could stop us at this point. "Oh, Thea, you come... with a friend -- rogue."

He looked between the two of us, then smirked in satisfaction. "He's the one that marked you. That's quite scandalous. I mean, the Alpha's daughter who lived as an Omega is sleeping with a rogue."

"And this rogue is going to watch you bleed to death." Josh pushed me aside and took threatening steps to Bryce.

"I've been itching for a fight," Bryce stretched his arms. My heart was speeding up the closer they got to one another.

"Everything you did to her..." Josh trailed on. I warned him to not fight out of anger. I needed him to stay concentrated so he could remain at an advantage.

"The sex was great, I cannot lie. The feeling of her skin on mine. Her body exploring every inch of mine as I explored hers." I shivered as Bryce described his experience with me. The feelings weren't mutual. Not in the least. Josh growled in anger and shifted.

'Focus,' I mindlinked Josh, but he had completely blocked me out. Bryce shifted after him, but Josh jumped on him before he had a chance to finish.

My heart was pounding in my chest and a sudden fear overcame me. I felt like everything was a bad idea. My mind was coming up with so many different ways we could have approached this. Anything but Josh getting hurt.

"Stop!" I yelled as Bryce kicked Josh back. I ran toward them, but Alexander grabbed me and held me back. "Let me go!" I cried angrily as tears fled from my eyes.

"You'll get hurt. They won't stop until the other is dead," Alexander explained.

"I don't care!" I hit his arm and wiggled around, but he had a tight grip on me. "Please!" I cried. "Josh!" As soon as I said his name, he turned toward me. Bryce took his moment of surprise to clamp down on his hind leg. Josh growled and turned back around.

"Thea, you're going to get him killed. There's nothing you can do now. Isn't this what you wanted?"

Isn't it what I wanted? For Josh to let out his anger on Bryce. As much as he wanted to fight for me, our battle was between Bryce and I. I dragged Josh along. I'm the reason he's in this position now. If I hadn't dragged him out of the snow... he'd already been dead. If I just let him leave after I healed him. If I did anything to get him out of harm's way. Is this really what I wanted?

"I... I don't know," I whispered stepping back.

"Thea! Oh God! I came as soon as I heard!" Riley stumbled over and hugged me. "Who-Who's winning?" She stared at the ongoing fight. It was hard to tell. They were both attacking one another equally as bad.

"I-I don't know, but I want it to stop! I want it all to stop! I'll do anything. I'll-I'll be the Omega. I'll let Bryce be Alpha. God, please!" I looked up at the sky, but in return, rain droplets fell on my skin and blended with my own tears.

I heard a yelp, and my head snapped to the action. Bryce was on top of Josh and bit into his neck. Blood squirted everywhere and Bryce fell back to the ground. "Josh!" I ran toward him, but Alexander stopped me. Josh shifted back and Bryce stood up to kill him off once and for all.

"No!" I ripped my arm from Alexander and ran toward Josh's body.

"Thea, no!" Riley rushed over after me, but I reached Josh. Bryce glared at both of us as I cradled his head in my lap. "Stop!" Riley stood in front of Bryce, and he didn't even attack her. He stared into her eyes.

"Josh," I whispered.

He opened his eyes and I met his dull gray eyes. I sighed in relief he was still breathing. I tore off a piece of my shirt and tried to wipe away the blood, but the bite was fatal. "Isn't this where we first met?" Josh whispered. I glanced at our surroundings. We were just outside the secret opening into my room. Pieces of glass scattered around the grass.

"Don't speak, you'll be okay," I whispered rocking him back and forth. He started to cough blood, and my heart constricted. "It's my fault-"

"No, it's.... it's.... not. I-I did... I did this," he sputtered.

"Josh, please, don't speak. Not until you're okay," I cried brushing away his hair. "Someone help! Anyone!" I wailed.

I looked up at Riley again to see that she and Bryce remained staring at one another as if they were having a silent conversation with their eyes. "I'm... not going to.." Josh coughed. His body went limp in my arms, but I continued to rock him.

"No," I cried holding him tighter. The life in his eyes had completely vanished.

I felt someone pulling me up, but I yanked away. The person was stronger and dragged me along. "No!" I yelled staring at Josh's limp body, then Bryce. Bryce. Still breathing. Still alive. My breaths became labored and heavy. I elbowed whoever was holding me back and when their grip on me loosened, I broke free and grabbed one of the shards in the grass. I held so tightly to it that it tore through my skin and I felt blood pouring down my arm, but I ignored it. I shoved Riley aside and swung my arm at Bryce. He dodged my first swing but looked back over at Riley. With all my remaining strength, I drove the knife into his fur, aiming for his heart.

"No!" Riley pulled me back, but she was too late. Bryce looked at her, then back at me with utter shock in his eyes. I was shaking with anger. His body fell to the ground with a loud thud, and Riley cried hysterically.

"I'm sorry," I whispered without any emotion.

"No," she wiped her tears away, "you did the right thing." She looked over at Bryce's body, and my gaze landed on Josh. He still didn't move. He was lifeless.

Is this the cost of freedom?

<h1 align="center">•Epilogue•</h1>

● Theadora Sanford•

'Luna, Ashton's cookies are ready!' Anna sang gracefully to me through mindlink.

'Have him bring them up to my office, please,' I requested.

Jake hummed a tune as he walked into my office, "Where's Tiger?"

"He'll be up in a minute. I don't appreciate you calling my son Tiger. He has the impression he actually is one," I frowned.

He laughed, "That's my bad, I suppose. We wouldn't want a Werewolf to think he's a tiger, let alone, an Alpha."

"Did you receive my E-mail?" I averted the subject.

"No. What E-mail?"

I swore, "I told one of the guards to send you one. It's blueprints for the addition to the house. I specifically told the guard to send Jake an E-mail," I grumbled.

"Well," he shrugged, "you have to say Beta, or else they'll send it to another Jake around the pack house."

I laughed, "Beta Jake. Still doesn't sound right."

He rolled his eyes, "By 5 years, I'd think you'd get the hang of it, Miss Luna."

"Mommy! Mommy!" Ash burst into the room and ran over. His green eyes were sparkling with excitement as he rushed over and hugged me.

"Hey, Tiger!" Jake growled playfully. I gave him a pointed look.

"Mama, look what I made!" He opened his hand to reveal crushed cookies and his hands were covered in chocolate. He gasped, "They weren't crumbled when Anna gave them to me!"

"We'll clean it up momentarily. Jake, I'll be more specific next time with the E-mails. May I have a minute?"

Jake nodded, "Sure thing. Goodbye Thea, bye Tiger."

Ash growled at him as if he were actually a tiger and I rolled my eyes. "Alright, Ash, let's go clean up." I picked him up. "Don't touch mommy with your chocolatey hands." Ash giggled and pointed a chocolate-covered finger in my face. I sat him on the bathroom counter and turned on the water. He splashed it all over me, and I huffed.

"Ash, mommy's going to kill you!" I growled.

"No, mama, please don't!" He held onto my shirt tightly.

"I'm kidding, baby. We're going to go see daddy today, okay?" I grinned at him as he finished washing his hands, despite the fact that he made a mess.

"Alright, mama. I picked the flowers today!" He exclaimed jumping down and grabbing my hand. "Come on, ma. Want to see?"

"Of course," I let him drag me out of the bathroom and down the hall. He excitedly bounced around. He was a very hyper child. Anna waved to the both of us as we passed the kitchen, and we made it to the gardening room. Bent over a few plants was Riley. She turned around to our arrival and Ash hugged her legs.

"Why, isn't it my favorite nephew?" She lifted him into her arms and kissed his cheek.

"Good afternoon, Aunt Riley!" Ash kissed her cheek back and cuddled himself to her neck. "Me and mama need flowers to go visit daddy."

She grinned and walked over to the cooling fridge, "I had the flowers saved just for you." Riley opened the fridge and pulled out a bouquet, "Aren't they lovely, Thea?"

I nodded, "The most beautiful I've ver seen." She handed them to me and I hugged her tightly. "Thanks, Rye."

She set Ash down and he ran back over to me. "Come on, ma!" He pulled my pants and I followed him.

"Visit some other time soon!" She waved, and I waved back to her. Ash slowed down as we reached the back door and I opened it for him. His excitement vanished within moments and he slowed down as we neared the gravesite

"Come on, baby," I took his hand and he whimpered as we reached the land filled with plots. Each name had its own story, but mine lived within the single one that was different from the rest.

Joshua Wiley

Ash stared for a minute, then ran over and hugged the cold stone. I grinned at him sadly and saw tears fall from his eyes. "It's okay, baby," I assured bending down and hugging him tightly. "Do you want to go back inside?"

He nodded against my hair, so I kissed his forehead and let him go back. I remained at the grave of my love and felt tears of my own grace my eyes. "He gets bigger and bigger every day," I whispered kneeling down to be at eye-level. "He has your smile... your hair," I went on to explain. "My mama's gorgeous eyes."

The wind spoke in return and blew at my skin. I pressed my teeth together and continued, "I remember when we first met. I was 16, I recall. Saved you from certain death, and it was the best decision I've ever made," I confessed. I cleared my throat and blinked back my tears. I didn't want to get choked up. "Gift, you told me. My name means gift, and God knows why you'd know such a thing." I tilted my head, "until I found the old records of this pack before Alexander took over. Theadora Wiley. She was your older sister. You never had the chance to tell me your full story, but I do know at one point in our childhood we must have crossed paths." I sighed and stared at the simple carvings on the stone.

Beloved rogue

Beloved lover

Beloved father

I bit my lip. I didn't want anyone to forget. Josh was a rogue, but he just wanted a home. A family. That was why he was so damn persistent in killing Bryce in the first place. Not all rogues are... horrible. "I did a little research myself, and I figured out what your name means," I placed the flowers on his grave and stood back up.

"Savior."

www.ingramcontent.com/pod-product-compliance
Lightning Source LLC
Chambersburg PA
CBHW070350200726
48294CB00003B/823